I0533551

IN THE SHADOW OF THE LOST WORLD

Ilko Minev

IN THE SHADOW OF LOST WORLD

Copyright © 2018 **Ilko Minev**
Translated by Diane Grosklaus Whitty

Published by Eriginal Books, Miami, 2019
www.eriginalbooks.com
www.eriginalbooks.net

ISBN-13: 978-1-61370-109-6
ISBN-10: 1-61370-109-8

All rights reserved. No portion of this book may be reproduced, stored in a retrieval system, or transmitted in any form or by any means—electronic, mechanical, photocopy, recording, scanning, or other—except for brief quotations in critical reviews or articles, without the prior written permission of the author.

More than a century ago, British writer Sir Arthur Conan Doyle, creator of the famous detective Sherlock Holmes, wrote *The Lost World*, inspired by the mystery of the alluring Mount Roraima

Contents

Lake Caracaranã

Traffic had gotten much heavier on the highway over the last few miles. Alice and I were finally reaching our destination: Lake Caracaranã, a favorite weekend spot for those living in the state of Roraima, where they could flee the scorching summer heat. I noticed a number of small planes tied down in a field alongside a makeshift landing strip. Not far away were a few chalets and a low structure, without any walls, that appeared to be a restaurant.

It wasn't easy to find a parking spot. Pickups were the most popular form of transportation around there, and more than a hundred of them were parked every which way near the building. There were no lines on the ground marking off stalls, and Alice had to help me maneuver into a tiny open space.

The restaurant was packed. People in no apparent hurry stood around waiting for a table while they enjoyed a beer and some conversation. We walked right by them all, heading straight to the white-sand beach. Someone clever enough to realize people would need refuge from the inclement tropical sun had planted cashew trees next to the native vegetation, and we found welcomed shade beneath their low boughs. The beach sloped gently to the transparent green waters of the placid lake. A steady breeze was blowing, and Alice and I watched in delight as a dozen windsurfers on colorful boards raced back and forth across the lake at amazing speeds. It was an almost magical sight, in stark contrast with the dry, drab yellow scenery more typical of this region of Brazil.

I walked over to a small brick building that looked like it might be the place to check in. Alice and I needed a chalet for the weekend. I opened the door and stepped into a room that appeared dark after the bright sun outside. Once my eyes had adjusted, I saw an elderly gentleman seated behind an old desk. He was short and thin and had a head of neatly combed-back gray hair. In a friendly voice, he introduced himself as Joaquim and told me they had no vacancies left that night. Many people, he said, actually planned to sleep in their trucks or camp out in tents. But he assured us it would be a different story the next day, with plenty of rooms opening up.

I was worried about Alice. Late in the fourth month of her pregnancy, after nearly three weeks of complete bed rest and all due precautions—and despite all our best efforts—she had lost our baby. It had been a terrible blow. Nearly a month had passed since that seemingly endless ordeal, and I knew she still hadn't recovered, although she tried valiantly to hide her sadness from me. I was worried she might sink deeper into depression, so I really wanted to provide her more comfort than the seat of a pickup. Joaquim, who explained he owned the inn, recommended a small bed and breakfast run by a woman named Dona Amélia in Normandia, a small town along the lower Maú River, where the grasslands meet the savannah, a few miles from Lake Caracaranã.

I insisted Alice relax in the clear, refreshing waters of the lake for a few hours before we drove to Normandia. It was just what she needed. We held hands for a long time, each of us lost in our thoughts. Lately, it seemed she didn't want to talk much, so we would often spend hours in silence, pondering our lives. This silent contemplation was good for me too. Two years earlier, I'd abandoned my mining dredge on the Madeira River. I could consider myself lucky; after all, I'd suffered only three cases of malaria—once for each year there—and my time under those harsh conditions had left only few marks on my body. I was living in a much different world than my homeland of Bulgaria, which was now far behind me, in Eastern Europe.

My name is Oleg Hazan and I was born in Sofia in 1948, not long after World War II. My father, David Hazan, was a Bulgarian Jew and my mother was Russian. As so often the case back in those days, my childhood was quite turbulent. First came my parent's stormy divorce, soon followed by a painful separation from my mother, who went back to Moscow to be close to her family. I saw her only once a year, during summer vacation. Then came my father's sudden fall from grace. After fighting for the resistance during World War II, he had become an important member of the Communist government plutocracy. And then, overnight, he was labeled a traitor and an enemy of the regime and was sent to prison for three harsh years. I lost my bearings after this abrupt, enormous change in my life. For a long time, it felt as if the ground had gone out from under me.

After my father's release from prison, we managed to cross the Iron Curtain and flee the Communist "paradise." We sought shelter in Israel, where I served in the Israeli Army and fought in the Yom Kippur War, a short-lasting but nonetheless horrendous experience. Then I earned my degree in engineering and embarked on a career.

In 1985, at the age of thirty-seven and at the invitation of my Uncle Licco, I immigrated to Brazil. I went to work at my cousins' company in Manaus and then at their branch office in Porto Velho. That's where I had my first contact with gold mining on the Madeira River—and where I caught the miserable gold fever. It wasn't long before I'd bought a dredge and turned myself into a prospector. I ran a small but relatively successful mining operation until the famous War of Prainha, when a huge band of thugs attacked the three-dredge convoy I was leading. With some luck, a good dose of bravado, and a lot of tenacity, we launched an overwhelmingly successful response to the attack, and I found myself a hero overnight, a kind of uncontested idol among the prospectors. Despite our victory and my fame, the incident left me disillusioned about prospecting. So, disillusioned in fact that I gave in easily to Alice, who wanted nothing more than to drag me away from that dangerous, surreal life. I sold my dredge and gave up prospecting.

The two of us moved to Manaus, where we opened a small river transport company that served the interior of the Amazon and nearby states. It wasn't long before our first son, David, was born. David bore the responsibility of honoring two remarkable people: my father, David Hazan, who had fought the Nazis and been a victim of power struggles inside the Bulgarian Communist Party, and my mother-in-law, a charming green-eyed woman with a mixture of indigenous and European ethnicity named Maria Bonita, who had survived a yellow fever outbreak in a lost rubber forest, deep in the state of Rondônia.

Dona Amélia's bed and breakfast was full, so we ended up staying in a four-room house next door, owned by Dona Benedita, the niece of Normandia's founding father. At dinnertime, the guests were forced to listen to Dona Benedita's interminable stories about the fascinating past of this distant, forgotten corner of Brazil.

It had all begun when Maurice Marcel Habert arrived in 1948, near the Wanamará River at the foot of the Serra do Cruzeiro mountains. Habert, an adventurer from France, was an experienced prospector as well as a blacksmith, locksmith, and skilled mechanic. He recognized the area's strategic value and also knew the land would be good for farming and cattle-raising. Without a second thought, he decided to settle there. He used the money he'd made prospecting to buy an entire ranch dirt cheap from a man who had served in Brazil's Expeditionary Force in World War II. Out of love for his homeland and in honor of the Allied landing on the French coast, he named the place Normandia, Portuguese for Normandy. He was so astute in selecting the location that a number of government agencies quickly set up offices there. They soon built a landing strip, followed by a health clinic, school, telegraph office, and police station. And so, Maurice Marcel Habert's property gave birth to the town of Normandia.

Our evening held many other surprises. As I listened to Dona Benedita's stories about her uncle's adventures, it felt like I was at the movies. I had read the book *Papillon* and seen the movie not long before. Henri Charrière, author of the novel, had escaped the hell of Devil's Island, a penal colony in French Guiana. His enthralling, realistic description of man's stubborn fight for freedom against any and all odds had captured readers around the world. Those of us seated around Dona Benedita's table were astonished to learn that the history of Normandia's founder rivaled that of Papillon's. After three frustrated attempts to escape, Habert, prisoner number 46841, who had been locked up in French Guiana since 1931, finally managed to escape, in the company of two others. The three of them eventually reached Georgetown, capital of what was then British Guiana. Driven by their fear of extradition to France and hoping to get as far away from the Guianas as possible, the three fugitives overcame their exhaustion and set off on a perilous, months-long trek through the jungle, crossing white water rapids and negotiating countless waterfalls. In 1941, nearly a year after their escape, the three adventurers entered Brazil, where they finally felt somewhat safe. They survived by doing menial labor on frontier ranches—until they discovered the Maú River, where gold prospecting had just begun. "The

Frenchman quickly found a spot and, in a few days, had gathered a 'hatful of' diamonds. The place is still known as Mauricio's Mine," said Dona Benedita, obviously very proud of her uncle. I hadn't been prospecting long myself before I had picked up the expression "hatful of," meaning to strike it rich in diamonds or gold.

Earlier that evening, I had noticed another dinner guest who, like me, was engrossed in the tales of the French adventurer. But I could tell it wasn't the first time he'd heard Dona Benedita's stories. I figured he must be a friend of the Habert family, maybe the owner or foreman of some cattle ranch. He was tall, tan, and muscular, with a face lit by a pair of blue eyes that contrasted with his indigenous features. Even more unusual was the head of dishwater blond hair sticking out from under his inseparable straw hat, which he didn't take off once during our meal. Although he looked like a fun-loving kind of guy, he had little to say and limited himself to nodding his head in agreement whenever the owner asked him to confirm something.

It was only after dinner, when we were all heading to our rooms, that Dona Benedita realized she hadn't introduced us. "This is Antônio Costa. He owns Santa Virgínia Fazenda, the biggest, finest farm on the Surumu River," she said.

"And to judge by your names and accents, you aren't from around here," the gentleman said.

"I'm Oleg Hazan," I replied. "This is my wife, Alice. She's from Rondônia. I'm from overseas, but I've been living in Brazil for six years."

I told him we'd been drawn to that part of Roraima by the region's natural beauty and the famous Lake Caracaranã. I also told him we wanted to relax a little after a few rough months, including my wife's complications with her pregnancy and her loss of our baby despite our best efforts.

That was how I met Antônio Costa. I couldn't imagine it was the beginning of a friendship fated to mark our lives. Even less could I imagine that within a few years, Normandia would be stage to dramatic events that would change our lives forever.

<hr/>

We got up early the next morning, but not early enough to say goodbye to our new acquaintances, who had already left. Before going back to the beach at Lake Caracaranã, we went to the edge of town and climbed the Serra do Cruzeiro mountains, where we looked down on the houses below. I imagined that on a sunny day you could see as far as Mount Roraima. Despite a steady wind, the heat started getting to us after lunch, so we said goodbye to Dona Benedita and returned to the comfort of the lake's green waters. It was Sunday afternoon and by some miracle, most of the visitors had vanished. There wasn't a single plane around, and only a dozen or so cars remained.

Joaquim, the inn's owner, quickly recognized me and offered us one of the now vacant chalets. Alice and I were planning on staying a few more days, so it was an irresistible invitation.

It was almost sunset, a time when many people enjoyed gazing across Lake Caracaranã, as the landscape underwent a breathtaking transformation. The sunlight reflected so brightly when it struck the water that it was hard to look directly at the lake. Normally light green, the water first grew darker and then slipped quickly through the colors of the rainbow, until turning reddish. At that exact instant, the big ball of fire that had been slowly descending behind the distant mountains lit the sky from a new angle, shifting the performance into the heavens. Pushed along by the region's steady winds, the few white clouds in the sky began changing shape and color, leaving the impression that everything around us was in constant movement. The show lasted only a few minutes, and then the sun simply vanished, but the sky remained illuminated a bit longer, until darkness fell.

〰〰〰〰〰〰〰〰〰〰〰〰〰〰〰

The empty restaurant seemed a lot bigger at dinner, since only one table was occupied when we got there. I recognized our new acquaintance and his family. I was just going to wave, but the tall man stood up, came over, and invited us to join them. We accepted. I was certain Alice would get along well with Conceição and Antônio; she always made friends easily. Conceição's belly was big and pointed, and she didn't stop running after their little girl, who was taking her first wobbling steps. The girl was an eye-catcher, with unusual coloring for that region of Brazil: blond hair and light green eyes, the color of the lake. She soon won Alice over. I realized that in some comforting kind of way my wife identified with the pregnant woman; after all, she should have been in the same situation.

Joaquim came over with the blueprints for some new bungalows he wanted to build. It was clear that Antônio and Joaquim Correa de Melo, owner of Caracaranã Fazenda, were close friends despite their age difference.

"Joaquim here was actually a very good friend of my late father, Mário," Antônio said. "Over 15 years ago, when it all started, my dad helped Joaquim and his son, Luiz Otávio, plan this inn. In the early years, there was a company that leased and managed the property, but the Correa de Melo brothers have been taking care of everything themselves more recently."

"Now it's my turn to reciprocate," said Joaquim, "and it's Antônio who's asking me for advice. He wants to build an inn something like mine on the Surumu River, on Santa Virgínia Fazenda."

Antônio proudly explained that he owned a quarter-mile-long, white-sand beach where an immense boulder projected into the river, right on the edge of his farm. He described it as a one-of-a-kind place of extraordinary natural beauty; its waters teemed with a wide variety of fish, making it a favorite spot for the regions' sportsmen.

I gave them some of my background too—my arrival in Brazil six years earlier, my first days in Manaus, and then my time in Porto Velho, where I had sold trucks and outboard motors, followed by the nearly three years I'd spent prospecting along the Madeira River.

"Around here, we've all been prospectors at least once in our lives," Antônio said with a smile. "My dad bought Santa Virgínia Fazenda in 1933 with money he'd made in diamond mining. The same thing happened with the Frenchman, Maurice Habert, who founded Normandia. Although he's been a cattle rancher for many years, Joaquim Correa de Melo, who has honored us with his presence tonight, has some experience in prospecting too. Not to mention, he was also in government for a while: deputy mayor and justice of the peace in Normandia. A lot of marriages were officialized in the 1970s thanks to him and him alone."

"Roraima is rich in ore, gold, diamonds, chromium, platinum, nickel, and even niobium," Joaquim said. "But now my work doesn't have anything to do with prospecting, public service, or politics—it's just my inn. Tomorrow I'm going to the ranch with Antônio and help him find the best spots to build the cabanas and other facilities. It's better to have a friendly competitor. I'm sure there's room for another inn. Roraima doesn't have hardly any resorts and Caracaranã can't handle everyone. And we don't have any plans to expand."

"What about you, gringo? Your wife and Conceição already look like old friends. Would you like to come with us? You'd get to see a bit more of our state. There's plenty of room in the main farmhouse and you can spend the night."

It was a welcomed invitation.

The Surumu River

We drove leisurely up state highway RR-319, which was nothing more than a poorly maintained gravel road. We were traveling in three king-cab pickups, a favorite vehicle in Roraima. We would have made better time if there were just one of us: Even though we kept a good distance from each other, the front truck raised so much dust that it slowed down the second, and the poor guy in third had real trouble seeing at all. Despite the strong winds blowing across the open fields, the dust seemed to hover lazily above the road. On either side of the highway, the dry, yellow grasslands of Roraima's savannah ecosystem, known as the *lavrado*, swept all the way to the horizon, broken only by a few scattered trees and bushes.

As we neared the Surumu River, Alice and I noticed the landscape shift into much greener colors, with some broad fields appearing too. In recent years, rice production had gained much ground and was revolutionizing the state economy. We passed a narrow side road with a sign indicating the way to Providência Fazenda; another sign soon showed the way to Tatu Fazenda. Then our three dust-covered trucks turned onto the bumpy road that would take us to Santa Virgínia. It was a rough ride, but we were nearing our destination.

"Driving here in rainy season must be awful, even with 4-wheel drive," I said. It occurred to me that access would need to be improved before anyone could even think about any kind of business ventures.

The road got better as we drove onto the property itself; it showed signs of ongoing maintenance. A few minutes later, we passed some horses on a small stud farm and then a well-tended vegetable garden. Next came a large field where a hundred or so head of Nelore cattle were grazing.

We arrived at the farmhouse dooryard, where an old truck and tractor were parked out front; neither appeared to have seen recent use. A large two-story stucco house was nestled into the hillside, overlooking the Surumu River. Antônio's car was soon surrounded by German shepherds. I counted six of them. An especially burly dog planted his front paws on the driver's side window. Antônio rolled it down and hugged the dog around its furry neck. You could tell there was a very tight bond between man and animal.

"Behave now, Sharo! We've got visitors. None of your threatening growls."

I thought I might have heard wrong. The dog's name tickled at something buried in my memory, but I didn't have a chance to ask any questions.

Alice was taking in the spectacular view at the far end of the farmyard. Beyond a carpet of lush vegetation lay a lovely river of dark, calm waters flowing alongside a beach of fine white sand, where a giant slab of dark stone jutted halfway into the river.

"My father was a gardener and for years his specialty was growing legumes, all sorts of varieties, back in Europe. He learned landscaping in Austria, specializing in flowers. That's why this farm looks like a well-groomed park. The only thing missing is a castle," said Antônio, who made no attempt to disguise his pride. "We have nearly 2,500 acres of top-notch soil, all legally registered. If you know how to plant things right and look after them, you're guaranteed bumper crops. Did you notice the rice fields on your way in? We harvest twice a year, and productivity around here meets that of Asia."

That same day, Alice and I got to see the rest of the property, took a swim in the river, and joined in the talks between Antônio and Joaquim. We were glad to share our own opinions about where to locate the dining hall and chalets of the future inn. We all agreed the best thing would be something along the lines of the inn on Lake Caracaranã, which had proven to be a good model. There was room enough for a large parking lot and the obligatory airport for small planes and ultralights. And there would be plenty of guests. Many prospectors abandoned the gold and diamond fields on the weekend to hunt down entertainment in the form of booze, women, and partying. Not to mention that people would come from Boa Vista, the state capital, and from Normandia.

The main farmhouse was airy and comfortable. A steady breeze kept it so cool that you didn't need air conditioning at night. A small generator supplied just enough energy for the lights and two refrigerators. I saw only one air-conditioner and it wasn't even turned on.

As if guessing my thoughts, Joaquim said, "You're going to need a large generator to provide power to all the bungalows—except, of course, during the days of Cruviana, goddess of the wind. According to legend, Cruviana turns into a chilly wind at night and seduces outsiders, who wake up so in love that they never again want to leave northern Brazil. We get that darn Cruviana on Lake Caracaranã too."

We talked late into the night. Antônio told us that his father, Mário Costa, had been just twelve when his mother died of tuberculosis. The two of them moved to Vienna, then the thriving capital of the Austro-Hungarian Empire. Four years later, his father passed away following a mysterious ailment the doctors weren't able to treat. Antônio again told us his father had been a skilled gardener, who first specialized in legumes but then started growing all kinds of flowers. He said his grandfather had had a fertile imagination and an incontestable eye for beauty, so it wasn't long before he was a famous landscaper. Before dying, he passed the profession down to his son, who suddenly found himself alone in the world. When a former client of his father's, a wealthy Portuguese diplomat, offered Mário a job, he decided to move to Portugal.

Mário was restless and didn't stay long in the city of Porto, where his benefactor lived. Although Antônio couldn't say for sure, he imagined that Mário's adventurous spirit accounted for his move to Brazil, even though he still spoke barely any Portuguese at that point. And he didn't move just anywhere in Brazil, but to the Amazon, in hopes of striking it rich with "black gold," the balls of rubber that were in growing demand around the world.

Antônio knew how to tell a story. He told us how his 18-year-old father had arrived in Belém, the natural port of entry to the mysterious Amazon, with hardly any money in his pockets back in 1912. He thought he was lucky when he landed a job right off the bat, even if it was only a contract on a rubber plantation on the distant Madeira River, right in the heart of the forest. The young adventurer had no clue he would be just another wretch on the famous ship *Justo Chermont*, a miserable vessel that delivered many Northeasterners, Portuguese, and other men in the prime of their youth into the humid, deadly arms of the jungle and into deprivation, humiliation, and slavery. Antônio struggled to hold back the tears welling up in his eyes. He also told us that his father, a trusting immigrant, couldn't imagine what awaited him on the rubber plantation. Labor was always in short supply there because the place was so isolated, so far from everything, and the mortality rate was high. In that surreal world, given the immeasurable sacrifices great numbers of unfortunate men had to make, the only ones who managed to amass immense fortunes were a handful of rubber barons and merchants (many of them Portuguese); they made lots of money on the production and sale of latex. They also took full advantage of another source of income by selling products and services to the tappers at exorbitant prices. The tappers began their lives in the Amazon by working to pay off their initial debt: their ticket from the Northeast, their rifle and ammunition, and other essentials. But they soon discovered their debt just kept growing, and they'd never be able to pay it off. They paid back so much and still owed so much more, eventually finding themselves veritable white slaves.

"A young Portuguese fellow by the name of Ferreira de Castro spent four long years on another rubber plantation in the same region. By a twist of fate, he had been another hapless passenger on the *Justo Chermont,*" Antônio said. "Even today, his book, *A Selva*—"The Jungle"—is the most accurate, moving account of that disgraceful period. My father never talked about those black years of his life. We never had many books here in the house, but ever since I can remember, we've had "The Jungle." I don't know where my father got the book, but I know it really meant something to him—he'd get teary-eyed whenever he leafed through it. I only read it recently and that's when I learned everything that happened in Amazon's rubber stands less than a century ago. It's hard to believe, but only now do I understood what my father felt when he read his own story in that book.

"My father and Ferreira de Castro must have led very similar lives for some time, even though they didn't meet until 1915, when my father, thanks to some superb luck and his athletic build, managed to escape the rubber plantation—on his first try and despite the risk of being tortured or shot in the back. As a young white slave, drowning in a debt that wouldn't stop growing, he was so desperate that he ignored the dangers and risked his life. Anyone who reads "The Jungle" understands this quickly."

I interrupted Antônio. "Can I ask you a question? What country was your father born in? Austria?"

"No, he was born in the late nineteenth century in a new country that had formerly been part of the Ottoman Empire for years: Bulgaria."

"That's what I thought," I said in a low voice. "When I heard your German shepherd's name, that's what I thought. Dogs are so often called Sharo in Bulgaria. Your father was a gardener in Vienna, was he? Of course, he had to be Bulgarian! In the late nineteenth century, hundreds of Bulgarian gardeners went to Austria to seek a better life. Believe it or not, Antônio, I'm Bulgarian too."

"So that's why we hit it off. Two Bulgarians lost in the far-off Amazon. It sounds like fiction." We were both pleased with our discovery. "For as long as I can remember, we've always had German shepherds here on the farm, and my father's favorite was always named Sharo. Every ten or fifteen years, when our special dog inevitably died, we'd pick out a puppy to be our new Sharo. Our current Sharo is one of the best we've ever had. Too bad he's getting old; he must be more than seven now. Our dogs are the best of their breed. We supply puppies to a number of other farms."

"Do you have any idea what your father's original name was?" I asked.

Without a word, Antônio got up and went into the next room. He came back holding an old folder with papers spilling out of it. "Here are all of my father's documents. Some are his

Brazilian records; others are written in German, as far as I can tell. And the others are in an alphabet I can't read—it must be Bulgarian."

I opened the folder and looked at the yellowed papers. Many were indeed in German, but others were in a language much more familiar to me: Bulgarian. They were written in the old script, one that isn't used anymore. It didn't take me long to find what I was looking for: "Marin Kostov, born on April 15, 1894, in Draganovo, Veliko Tarnovo." In Bulgaria, of course!

Santa Virgínia

〜〜〜〜〜〜〜〜〜〜〜〜〜〜〜〜〜〜〜〜〜〜〜〜〜〜〜〜〜〜〜〜

"I was thinking how much I'd have to invest to transform Santa Virgínia into an inn, and it occurred to me that I should lease out part of our property. Our neighbors are rice growers and I'm sure they'd be interested in buying, but I'd rather not sell. If I took my savings and added what I could make leasing some land, I could work on building an inn about the same size and quality as the one in Caracaranã."

Antônio was sharp. He'd realized that Alice had fallen in love with Santa Virgínia and that my questions suggested I might be interested in investing there. So he cut to the chase: "Would you two be interested in renting part of our little paradise? I'd love to have you as neighbors." Only two Bulgarian-Brazilians could be so frank with one another so soon after meeting.

I would eventually get used to Antônio's hard-hitting style, but right then, it felt a bit like he was pressuring me. I took my time answering and measured my words carefully. I explained that after losing our baby, we were indeed thinking about looking for opportunities far from big urban areas, at least for the time being. "Alice was born and raised among the rubber trees on the Abunã River in the state of Rondônia, and she loves life in the countryside. She misses more direct contact with nature. This might actually be a good opportunity," I said.

"So give some thought to investing here. This corner of Brazil, north of the equator, is rich and beautiful, but it's also mostly unheard of, and mostly ignored. Someday it will blossom. Land values haven't appreciated much yet, but it won't stay that way long. To tell the truth, I wouldn't lease any of our land if it wasn't for my dream of building a nice inn."

I had to admit the place was gorgeous. I really liked what I'd seen so far, but I had no idea what I could do with this vast area of land. Should I go into rice farming? And then there was this business of demarcating the territory and putting all the land into a new indigenous reserve—which would push all the farmers out. Antônio had a quick response when I broached the subject: "If you go back over my family's records since 1933, plus our registration with Brazil's land reform agency, INCRA, you'll see that the land inarguably belongs to us. My father bought it from the first owners, who came here during the Brazilian government's big settlement drive, around the time of the great Northeast drought of 1877. We're the legitimate owners, no doubt about it. And besides, we're mixed ethnicity. My mother was a Wapishana Indian."

Many Boa Vista residents were saying that the rumors about establishing a reserve called Raposa Serra do Sol were nothing but hot air and that a lot of the speculation came from people who simply didn't know what they were talking about. Some of them just wanted to create friction between the farmers and Indians. Everything indicated that when it came time for action, good sense would prevail.

We sat there a while in silence. I said I wanted two weeks to think it over and make sure it was feasible for us. Antônio was fine with that. I could tell he truly wanted me as a partner.

Antônio went on to regale us with some of the intriguing history of the pioneers who settled Roraima's *lavrado* region and began farming there in the late nineteenth century. A good many had lost their hearts to some lovely indigenous girl. According to Antônio, the legendary Severino Pereira da Silva— better known as Severino the Miner, one of the region's first gold prospectors—and the indigenous woman Simaria had dozens of children and hundreds of grandchildren, great-grandchildren, and great-great-grandchildren. They had lived in the mountain region for centuries. While most of the settlers came from the Northeast, some came from Europe, like the German and Dutch, and even a few from Japan. And they inevitably married native Brazilians.

"Someday I'll introduce you to Nelson Doy's descendants. Nelson was born in Japan. Can you imagine the result of mixing Japanese ethnicity with Northeastern and Indian?" Antônio had gotten on to his favorite topic.

The two of us were sitting on the farmhouse porch, enjoying the view of the Surumu River. We watched Alice and Conceição cross the beach and head toward the big rock.

"Let's join them," I said. "Maybe this is something we'll be doing a lot in the future." We both laughed.

We caught up to our wives at the far end of the rock, out in the middle of the river. I could understand why the local fishermen found the site ideal. Here they could cast off in all directions, toward the most promising spots. It would be hard to imagine a better location for a good caster equipped with a fine rod and reel. The inn would no doubt be a success. And this would make an outstanding tourist attraction.

~~~~~~~~~~~~~~~~~~~~~~~~~~~~

Bad as the road was before we reached the state highway, our trip back to Boa Vista went smoothly. Alice and I were quiet at first, but it was evident how eager we were to discuss Antônio Costa's unexpected offer. We'd fallen in love with the untamed beauty of Santa Virgínia, and we both thought the area was breathtaking. The soil was apparently quite rich as well, to judge from the neighboring rice fields and the garden planted by

Mário Costa. We would have to evaluate the cost of turning part of the property into a profitable rice farm. Although we still had some questions, we'd come to a decision by the time we reached Boa Vista: we would take the plunge and change our lives. We would take advantage of the next few years, before our three-year-old son David entered school, to realize our dream of leading a peaceful life in the country, surrounded by exuberant nature.

Faster than we could imagine, Santa Virgínia Fazenda was divided in three parts. The central area, near the main farmhouse, would become the inn. The area to the left of the entrance would be reserved for a parking lot, aerodrome, the main pasture for horses and Nelore cattle, and a small but flourishing vegetable garden. The other side of the property, where it would be easier to irrigate, would be devoted to rice. Alice promptly named our enterprise Shalom Rice Fields.

When we went to sign the lease, we were impressed by all the records Mário Costa had so carefully compiled and safeguarded. The oldest one showed the name of the first owner of the land, which had been occupied since 1877. His heirs had sold it in January 1933 to the second owner, Mário Costa; there was a deed dated that year. The property had also been registered at the deed's office in Boa Vista in 1954. The title indicated the precise location of Santa Virgínia—not common practice back then. The deed was accompanied by numerous other INCRA-issued documents. It was all very official and legal, and duly registered with INCRA. The fazenda was part of Mário Costa's estate, passed on to his only heir, his son Antônio. The records couldn't have been in better order.

To make it work, we all agreed that Alice, David, and I would stay in the main farmhouse the first year while we built our own place near the chalets and set up our rice operation.

The latter proved easy, since there was plenty of skilled labor around. The Indians who lived in nearby huts already had experience on other fields. We were excited when the first rice plants sprouted from the soil less than a year later. Meanwhile, our small home was taking shape; it would have three bedrooms, a living room, and a kitchen. Work on the inn was underway too, and the fact that we were buying construction material for two projects helped move things along. Even so, it wasn't easy to build on the Surumu River. Materials had to be brought from a distance, mostly from Manaus but also from as far away as São Paulo.

Roraima didn't have much to offer in the way of leisure opportunities, and it was interesting to see how quickly the inn became a success. Within a few months of opening, Antônio had four or five planes at the makeshift aerodrome and at least a couple dozen pickups in the parking lot every weekend. He fixed his old tractor so it could do non-stop maintenance of the road, now in much better shape. During those long hard days of work—and excitement—Alice would measure the Costa family's success every week by counting the empty beer cases waiting to be refilled on Monday.

After we planted the second year, we harvested our first substantial rice crop, and it looked like things would go even better in the future.

We had visited much of the region by then, including the nearby indigenous village that almost abutted Shalom, as well as some other fazendas in the area. The best-managed, most productive rice fields were those on the Canadá, Depósito, Tatu, and Providência fazendas on the Surumu River; Carnaúba Fazenda, where the Surumu and Tacutu rivers met; and Realeza Fazenda, on the Tacutu River. There were also some other, smaller farms in the lowland regions of the Cotingó River.

Although rice had only arrived in the region about fifteen years earlier, it was already one of the most important economic forces in Roraima, with sales guaranteed to the neighboring states of Amazonas and Pará.

We abided by one of the region's traditions: Once a month, the Indians came in through the fence and carried off a steer to meet their community's needs. Nearly all the farmers went along with this, as a kind of good neighbor policy. It was a small price to pay for peace. Since Alice and I didn't have any cattle, we paid Antônio the equivalent of half a steer once a month. We got along fine with the Indians back then. Some of those from the nearby village worked in the rice fields. It seemed like our good relations would continue well into the future. Our constant contact with our indigenous neighbors sparked our curiosity. We wanted to learn more about their way of life and about what they thought.

Alice had known some Indians when she was a child, living in the rubber forests of Quatro Ases, but she only had a vague recollection of them. Her adoptive mother, Maria Bonita, didn't hide the fact that she had descended from a tribe on the Purus River, but she hadn't ever lived with them and didn't speak their language. I'd known some Indian prospectors in Rondônia, but my contact with them had always been superficial.

Right about the time our second rice harvest rolled around, Alice's mother and her husband Roberto moved to Boa Vista, and of course they became frequent visitors to Santa Virgínia Inn. Roberto had been a professor of history at the University of Glasgow and had finally gotten a professorship at the Federal University of Roraima. His Amazonian wife was thrilled to trade the cold European winters for the warmth of Brazil. For Alice, it was a breath of fresh air to have her mother so close by. Roberto got his hands on some books about the history of

Roraima, along with some papers and dissertations by university professors, and we devoured them. Now that this was our home, Alice and I had to know more about the state's history.

We read up on the settlement of the Branco River Valley—a reprehensible story that bore much in common with the history of the settlement of the Amazon. Down through the centuries, as civilization blazed its way into new lands, labor power had inevitably been in short supply. The solution had always been some form of slavery, either of blacks from Africa or of Indians, easily found and captured. Since the Africans came from far away and were expensive, the Indians in Roraima were stuck with the harsh job of serving the settlers who were exploring the territory.

There were many parallels between the development of the Amazon during the rubber days and the settlement of Roraima's *lavrado* region. Roraima was part of the state of Amazonas for centuries, and only became a federal territory in 1944. As a result of slave trafficking—a common practice throughout Portuguese America—countless indigenous groups from the Branco River Basin had been torn apart and practically decimated. The European colonizers treated the Indians like savage, soulless beasts. According to official records, the Portuguese Crown legalized the enslavement of Indians in 1611 and abolished it in 1775; however, mistreatment continued much longer. Throughout these years, Indians were moved against their will to communities and villages far from their homes, never again to return to life with their own people. They were enslaved, manipulated, and exploited by the clerics and *capitães de aldeia* in charge of mission villages, who presented themselves as their saviors.

We were appalled when we discovered that one form of cruelty after another had been practiced during settlement of the Branco River Valley. Indigenous people were treated like beasts of burden, and the women were often left to the sordid fate of serving as sex slaves. The natural aftermath had been a series of bloody revolts and clashes between Indians and settlers. Through our conversations with Roberto, Alice and I learned of three major rebellions. The last one took place in 1798 and culminated with the Blood Beach massacre, a slaughter that reddened the waters of the Branco River—which means "white river." Dubbed a "just war," this shameful, cowardly display of force by the Portuguese had disastrous consequences, with the Indians migrating en masse to what was then British Guiana. It was years before the Branco River saw the return of any economic activity. Exploration of rubber and balata gum began in the late nineteenth century along the lower Branco, close to its confluence with the majestic Negro River. Work was done by semi-slaves, mainly the Macuxi and Wapishana peoples, who still lived in the region, albeit now in lesser numbers. The Northeast drought of 1877 pushed a large wave of migrants to the Amazon. Official Brazilian government policy then focused on solving the drought problem while encouraging rapid settlement of unpopulated areas. Once Alice and I had familiarized ourselves with this historical background, it was easier for us to understand why so many land deeds dated to that period and why so many male settlers had married female Indians.

When we first moved to Roraima, I really couldn't tell one tribe from another. Over time, my interest grew, and I decided to do some research. I asked everyone who seemed to know about these things, and now I have a relatively good understanding of the origins, customs, and past of these peoples. I estimate that there are about 19,000 Indians from five ethnic groups living in the vicinity of Raposa Serra do Sol—Land of the Fox and Mountain of the Sun. Most are Macuxi, who are highly acculturated. The still-savage Ingarikó live around Serra do Sol; they have only sporadic contact with Army soldiers, prospectors traveling through their lands, and FUNAI, the government agency in charge of indigenous affairs. Then there are the Wapishana, Patamona, and Taurepangue, all of whom have their own unique characteristics and different degrees of acculturation. Roberto explained to us that the indigenous peoples in the Amazon basin come from three ethnic groups who speak different languages: Tupi, Arawak, and Carib. During the battles at the time of discovery, European invaders hunted down the Taurepangue and Macuxi (the latter form the largest group today), and so these indigenous people fled the Caribbean, following the Orinoco River basin. The Taurepangue and Macuxi engaged in bloody intertribal wars, driving out or simply decimating other tribes along the way, like the Wapishanas, who speak a language belonging to the Arawak group. The Macuxi were the first to use firearms, and they had no trouble winning a series of wars against the ethnic groups who dared defy them.

It was only after we had gained a better grasp of this history that we realized the wounds of the past hadn't fully healed and that strong feelings of animosity between settlers and Indians would return with time. To make matters worse, instigators could be found within a number of NGOs and even some federal agencies. Lastly, some settlers showed little understanding of the situation or displayed outright racist attitudes, although many others lived in peace and harmony with the indigenous peoples around them. All this was a source of worry, since we were truly enjoying our new life.

After some years of what could be called peaceful coexistence between settlers and Indians, it was predictable that major clashes would arise over the final demarcation of the Raposa Serra do Sol indigenous reserve.

Raposa Serra do Sol

Much faster than we could imagine, Santa Virgínia Inn became a popular vacation destination for people from Boa Vista and prospectors crisscrossing the skies of Roraima in their small planes. Weekends were busy and, as might be expected, we ran into problems with guests who drank too much. One day, the *tuxaua*, or chief, from the local indigenous village approached Antônio Costa to complain about guests often trespassing on their nearby land. That's when I first met the old *tuxaua* Genival, who proved to be a wise and earnest fellow. We talked a good while, long enough for me to tell him how we'd first visited Roraima and fallen in love with Santa Virgínia Fazenda. I also told him that we'd lost our baby and that Alice had finally gotten over it when we traded our lives in the city for the fazenda. By the time Genival and I said goodbye, it felt as if we'd known each other for ages. I was certain the two of us were going to get along well. Just before he left, the old man suddenly interrupted our casual chit-chat and pulled me aside. He called Antônio over too, and told us nervously: "Canaimé has grown strong again. There's going to be war and this time the Indians will win. We'll win, but it'll be bad for us and for the white man."

I waited until Genival had left and then asked Antônio who this Canaimé guy was.

"It's an old legend," he explained. "He's a being who's feared by the Indians, and by many of us too. Everything bad is caused by this cannibal, who's an evil half-man, half-beast.

Some people think he's not a single individual but a tribe of descendants of the god of evil. Whatever the case, the chief is predicting hard times."

I don't know why, maybe because of his calm voice, the *tuxaua* reminded me of the legendary statesman from India, Mahatma Gandhi. They didn't look at all alike, but I couldn't get the feeling out of my head.

Late the following afternoon, Alice and I went to nearby Pedra Grande, as we often did on weekdays when there were no guests. I enjoyed fishing at that magical spot at sunset, when the big star seemed to plunge into the waters of the Surumu River. Fishing was actually just a pretext. Alice and I always used the time to talk and cuddle a bit, while we gazed at the sunbeams reflecting off the dark waters of the river, like so many shards of glass, making it hard even to see.

We were transfixed by that explosion of light. Suddenly, I noticed a shadow coming toward us across the water. I could eventually make out a man standing upright in a small dugout. He was holding a bundle about the size of a shoe box, while someone else sat in the back rowing. Only when they reached the rock did I recognize *tuxaua* Genival, who waved at us as the canoe pulled alongside. He stepped out onto the rock and, without saying a word, handed Alice the small bundle in his arms, wrapped in a well-worn T-shirt. My wife's jaw dropped as she stared down at the bundle in incomprehension: there lay a small being, stirring and fussing—a tiny newborn, its face covered in bug bites.

"Your *curumim* died, Dona Alice, and your home is sad. There's no baby crying for the breast. I brought this little *curumim* for you, and I brought my niece, Araci, who has lots of milk. The *curumim* is yours. Take good care of him. He's weak and tiny." The *tuxaua* spoke in a solemn voice.

Alice was so shocked that she didn't know what to do. She looked at the baby, and then at me, hoping I'd somehow come to her rescue.

"Does it belong to your niece?" she asked softly.

"No, the *curumim* belongs to another girl. A prospector came through and then left. The girl can't take care of him. My niece can stay with you a few days to help out. If the baby stays with his mother, he'll die," the *tuxaua* said emphatically.

The baby started fussing. Alice unwrapped the T-shirt and stared down at the little creature, and at the bite marks covering his body. You couldn't tell the color of its eyes, which still couldn't see properly. Feeling the warmth of Alice's arms, the baby settled down. Some strange force seemed to unite the two of them, and I could see that Alice was trembling uncontrollably.

"We'll keep him." Her instinctive reply came in a quiet voice, nearly a whisper. A decision had clearly been made. That was what Alice wanted. At the same instant, I realized that not only did I have another child—my beloved wife had found her way of healing.

"May God help us!" was the next thought that shot through my head.

The *tuxaua* helped his niece out onto the rock and then quickly got back into his dugout. He rowed away slowly; his strokes strong for a man his age. In a few minutes, he had vanished around the river's bend. And that's how Alice and I found ourselves with our second son, Benjamin.

"He must be an unwanted baby," Antônio declared when he saw the tiny boy. He told us that sometimes when an indigenous baby is born to a naïve young girl who had a short-lived relationship with a virtually unknown man, the child isn't welcome and will be abandoned somewhere far from the village, because the mother won't be able to care for it. That accounted for the numerous insect bites. The rest of the tribe knows what's happening, but they look the other way and don't do anything about it.

"This is how some tribes have traditionally gone about things. Genival has a good heart, and he no doubt remembered you two and decided to save this little guy," Antônio said.

~~~~~~~~~~~~~~~~~~~~~~~~~~~~~~~~

It took the baby over two weeks to put on weight and acquire a healthy glow. As he recovered, I could feel Alice blossoming.

Everyone's routine changed with the addition of the newest member of our family. Alice kept busy with the baby during the day, and I would come back from the fields to eat lunch at home.

While our family was enjoying this happy phase, our rice crop was doing well too. It had practically doubled in a year and the outlook was for further growth.

One of the first things we learned was that we'd not only need a four-wheel drive truck to get around, on and off the plantation, but we'd need the four hooves of a good horse as well. Learning to ride was mandatory, and an entirely new experience for both of us. Antônio proved to be an excellent teacher. The aches and pains that we felt at the end of each training session began to abate after some months of trotting and galloping. We came to the conclusion that this was the most fun part of life on the fazenda. After horseback riding became one of our prime forms of entertainment, I went to

Boa Vista and bought three Mangalarga mares, taking Antônio's advice.

"Why do you only recommend mares?" I asked him. I couldn't figure it out. "I've noticed you've only got female horses too. Why the discrimination?"

"You'll understand this 'discrimination' soon enough," he replied with a smile.

A few days after the animals arrived, Antônio invited us to take a horseback ride beyond the borders of the fazenda. It was the first time we'd ever ridden so far. We were captivated by the wild nature around us. The plains seemed endless. They were blanketed by yellowed, basically dry grass, stretching for miles to the distant mountains and interrupted solely by a smattering of small trees, so barren they offered hardly any shade. Strange shapes rose up at the feet of most of these trees, in the limited shelter they provided from the inclement sun: they were huge termite mounds, almost as tall as their protectors. Hundreds or perhaps thousands of these structures lay as far as the eye could see. For virtually all living beings, except perhaps termites and anteaters, this enormous territory would be totally inhospitable, essentially a desert.

"It's remarkable, and actually mindboggling, that these steppes are part of the Amazon. The climate here, the topography, and other features are so different from the rest of the highlands, which are covered by the thick jungles that surround the Amazon and its branches," I said as we rode by the huge termite mounds.

"This desolate landscape changes completely during the rainy season, from April to September, when the lowest part of the plains is covered with a shallow layer of water because there's no drainage," said Antônio. "This summertime desert that we're looking at now turns into an enormous lake in the winter."

It was amazing to think we were only a few miles from the Surumu River. The landscape was so very different. We knew the topography changed again to the north, near the Tepuis, the mountain range capped off by tablelands, site of the famous Mount Roraima. Our plans included a trip to this mysterious mountain, renowned for its incomparable beauty.

Then I detected the shadow of a large animal moving among the giant termite mounds.

"Don't make a sound," Antônio whispered so softly I could hardly hear him. "We got lucky. There's a herd of *lavradeiros* right in front of us, behind the termite mounds. You're going to see something extraordinary now, and you'll understand why we buy only mares."

We carefully edged forward to higher ground so we could see more of the *lavrado*. There stood a herd of about ten horses, all quite small, their long manes unkempt.

"*Lavradeiros!* The wild horses of Roraima! I'd heard of them but never thought I'd ever see them up close." Alice was thrilled.

"Actually, when I invited you to go riding, I knew the horses were here. 'Peasant radio' works real good around here," Antônio joked. "We won't be able to get any closer because they're very skittish. They'll gallop off as soon as they spot us."

Continuing in a low voice, Antônio said, "Even though the wild *lavradeiros* of Roraima eat nothing but dry grass, they're super resistant, much more so than the Mangalarga and other pure breds. The horses stand barely five feet tall, but they can travel great distances at high speeds. During droughts, they have to travel days to find water. And in the rainy season, they go months with their hooves sunk in the layer of water covering the *lavrado*. That's probably why their hooves are so hardy. And that's where they get their nickname: 'hard foot'."

"I read somewhere that the *lavradeiros* descend from horses brought over by the Portuguese more than three hundred years ago," I said. "But I still don't understand why we buy only mares."

Antônio laughed as he revealed his secret. "These horses usually travel in herds of eight to ten females, with only one male. The lone stud is so macho that he services all his mares and still goes after the ones he meets along the way."

Antônio explained that his mares were all products of breeding *lavradeiros* with Mangalargas over and over. This meant he had resistant horses that boasted all the qualities of the pure Roraima breed. All you had to do was take your mares that were in heat and turn them out near the herd. The randy *lavradeiro* stud would say thanks and cover them immediately.

My Mother

Something else had a big impact on our families around that same time: a return to personal contact with my mother, Irina, quite some time after my father's sudden death.

Although we'd been apart for twenty long years, I'd kept in touch with my mother via letter. We hadn't seen each other since shortly after my parents' divorce, because my mother moved back to Moscow and I stayed with my father in Sofia, where I was studying physics at St. Kliment Ohridski. Although my parent's marriage had fallen apart, they harbored no resentments or hard feelings. It seemed likely to turn into another story of a friendly divorce where a grown child spends time with both parents. But nobody could imagine that shortly after their divorce, during yet another power shift in the Communist regime, my father would be accused of divulging some of Bulgaria's technological secrets to private companies in the West, ousted from his important government post, and imprisoned for nearly three years. After my father had served his sentence, he and I made a dramatic escape from the Communist "paradise," crossing the Iron Curtain and finding shelter in Israel. My mother had no direct involvement in any of this but watched the story unfold from afar. Throughout my college days in Israel, three years in the Army. And then my time prospecting on the Madeira River in Rondônia, she and I exchanged a steady stream of correspondence (I'm sure the KGB was aware of everything we wrote)—but there was never any chance we could meet personally. Although Irina suffered the pain of being separated from her child, she was still young and attractive, and she ended up remarrying, starting a new family, and rebuilding her life.

Then, nearly fifteen years after my father's arrest and just two years after his death, a miracle happened: the world watched incredulously and with heart in hand as the horrendous Berlin Wall came down and the Soviet Union vanished. When this harsh, oppressive regime met its demise, it meant my mother and I could finally think about meeting again.

In early May 1994, in the middle of Roraima's rainy season, when work on the rice crop almost grinds to a halt, and while the frigid Russian winter was giving way to a colorful spring, I set off on the long trip from the interior of Roraima to Russia. Our children were still too young for such a long adventure, so they stayed behind on the fazenda with Alice, in the company of the Costas. When people from Roraima travel, Manaus is always a mandatory layover. I'd been so busy with our rice crops that I hadn't ventured outside the state in a good long while, so this would give me a chance to spend a family Shabbat with my Uncle Licco and cousins Daniel and Sara. Everybody wanted to hear news about Alice and the children, and they were also curious about my new enterprise.

It was wonderful to feel part of a big family. Life on the fazenda was certainly pleasant, but it could also be quite lonely. I was happy to be back among loved ones, people who wanted what was best for me. In my new life, I had found myself needing advice, suggestions, and solutions that very few people could provide. I knew we'd soon have to make some changes in our habits and life style very soon if we were to give our children a solid education. What was even more challenging than their schooling was maintaining our Jewish traditions in the isolated world of the Roraima *lavrado*. Santa Virgínia

Fazenda was our home—for the time being. We had everything we needed, but in a little while our needs would be quite different.

"And the controversy over demarcation?" asked Uncle Licco, who, despite his age, kept up on the news.

I told them that controversy was inevitable if we were to arrive at a solution that ensured everyone's safety and made sense to both Indians and non-Indians. I pointed out that Roraima still lacked a solid economic foundation, since virtually everyone worked for some type of government agency, either federal, state, or local. It didn't take a genius to realize this wasn't a good practice, and that this distorted model would eventually exact a steep price. To make matters worse, indigenous reserves already occupied more than half the territory, and almost nothing was being produced on this land.

"As far as production goes, Roraima is the lowest-ranking state," said Daniel, who had a good understanding of things in Brazil's newest state. "Every single resident depends on the government and even though the region is extremely rich in minerals and has tremendous agricultural potential, sustainable economic activity like rice growing is new to Roraima."

Daniel was not at all confident that the Court's decision would be influenced by the need to create jobs and produce wealth. As he saw things, Brazil boasted such enormous natural riches that this effectively offset any government mismanagement. I had to agree. Our elites hardly ever encouraged productive activities or the creation of wealth anywhere. You'd think the quality of life we'd all like to enjoy was a right and not something to be won daily on the basis of everyone's hard work. You'd think you'd only have to write this into the Constitution, and everyone would automatically be guaranteed this benefit with a wave of a magic wand.

"We've got our own economic troubles here in Manaus," said Uncle Licco. "For years, the Free Trade Zone disguised things. There was no economic activity driving our state forward, other than the assembly plants they set up under the Trade Zone's fiscal incentives. With a few, laudable exceptions, the interior of the Amazon is a huge economic void, with neither a present nor a future."

It was evident my cousins were quite concerned about the future of Manaus's Free Trade Zone, which could only be sustained in the long run if Brazilian taxes remained high. In ten or twenty years, if Brazil was to be a modern, thriving country, taxes would have to be lowered. As Brazil adopted more of a free-market approach, the state of Amazonas, which depended heavily on these taxes, would no longer have a viable economy unless something were done about it.

"We've done nothing to prepare for what lies ahead, and one fine day we might find ourselves back to being a lumber port." Daniel's worry was shared by all.

I talked a little about my experiences in the Amazon and my ongoing concern about the absence of any medium- or long-term regional economic planning. Rather than pursuing sustainable development through planned, licensed, and regulated economic projects, it seemed we liked to just let things happen. Instead of mining, we seemed to prefer prospecting, with its crude, inefficient methods, high environmental costs, and no enforcement of regulations. And Brazil's environmental protection agencies apparently refused to do their jobs; instead of conducting inspections, they simply banned any productive activity, and this effectively jeopardized the preservation of the Amazon.

"The most glaring example is the Manaus-Porto Velho highway, which would be the only land link between

Amazonas, Roraima, and the rest of Brazil," Licco said with a sigh. "The so-called responsible agencies don't allow maintenance work on the existing stretches of road. They argue that if the road starts operating like it should, this would have a negative impact on the forest. The implication is that our environmental agencies don't feel they're capable of carrying out their natural job, doing surveillance in the region around the road. Even if this means a few million people pay the price of isolation."

Uncle Licco was voicing the shared unhappiness of people living in the Amazon, who felt Brazil's public policies had no basis whatsoever in an informed understanding of the region. We all knew that the Amazon's incredible biodiversity could provide new medicines, new cosmetics, and who knows what else—not just for the locals, who needed jobs, but also for the rest of humanity. But the false guardians of the forest invented so much red tape that nothing ever got off the drawing board.

"What does our judge have to say?" I asked. My cousin Sara was a family court judge for the state of Amazonas, and I wanted to hear her opinion.

"Well, getting back to the question of Raposa Serra do Sol, I think the solution will ultimately come from the courts," Sara replied. "Oleg, you're not going to like this, but the Brazilian government increasingly favors the continuous demarcation option. The thesis that 'the land belongs to the Indians, and all the others are invaders' is gaining ground."

"But," I argued, "the 'invaders' were settled there by this very same Brazilian government more than a hundred years ago. Many of them were born on those lands and they've got plenty of documents just as official and legal as the ones you have on your house here in Manaus."

"Right!" Daniel jumped in. "Our government authorities wouldn't dare apply these rules in Rio de Janeiro or São Paulo, but in Roraima—in these far-off fields north of the equator, where there aren't many folks to complain—they've got a unique opportunity to show the world how progressive, generous, fair, and politically correct we are in how we treat our Indians."

"That's just what my friend Antônio Costa and I didn't want to hear," I said, still loathe to accept these facts.

"Well," Sara said, "there's a strong feeling of guilt and regret about the heinous acts that all institutions—the church included—have committed against the Indians over the centuries. This will weigh heavily in court rulings. So it's quite likely that what seemed impossible a few years ago will come to pass. The judges will be hard pressed to hand down any true form of justice."

Uncle Licco was even more pessimistic. "From what I've read in the papers, everything suggests there will be justice for some and injustice for others."

I had to agree. But I didn't want to talk about this thorny topic anymore. So I turned to the subject of my upcoming trip to Moscow to visit my mother. I told them how nervous I was about seeing her again, after a twenty-year separation. And for good reason! Time had flown. First Israel: a new country, a new language, new friends; my time in the Army there, a war; college. Then Brazil: the Portuguese language, the Amazon, prospecting, marriage, children, and, last, our rice fields on the Surumu River. It had gone by so quickly. It had certainly been worth it, but in this race against time, my mother had grown ever more distant, even though she was always on my mind. Now she was my top priority.

I flew first from Manaus to São Paulo for a connecting flight. By the time I set foot on Russian soil at Domo-dedovo, one of Moscow's four airports, I had racked up forty hours in airports and airplanes. My reunion with my mother and my half-brother, Aleksei, 18 years younger than me, was very emotional. The last time I'd seen my mother, my brother hadn't even been born. Over the course of those many years, Irina (I couldn't decide if I should call her mom or Irina) had aged hard. She still had striking blue eyes, but her once lovely face was now heavily wrinkled—the same face that had bewitched a young Bulgarian student, my father, David Hazan, forty years earlier. Life obviously hadn't been easy on her. While I too had suffered the effects of the years, changing from boy to man, she recognized me immediately. We held each other close in a long embrace, not saying a word. She strained to hide her tears. Even though so many years had passed, I could identify and understand each sob. I couldn't hold back my own tears. It had been a long time since I'd cried. I hadn't cried when I lost friends in the Yom Kippur War, or when I said Kaddish for my father, or even when Alice lost our baby. But it was very different now. My mother, young and strong in my memory, had grown smaller and incredibly vulnerable. Standing in the middle of the crowded airport, we shed tears for all the years we could never bring back.

Moscow was still remarkably familiar to me. Even though the city was going through an unprecedented crisis, it still retained its majestic air. The Russian economy had actually gone backwards since the collapse of the Soviet Union, and it hit one of its lowest points in 1994. We walked along the Moskva River and Boulevard Ring for hours and visited the city's most popular tourist spots that week. I got a room on Red Square near the Kremlin, at the Moskva Hotel, a relic from the days of Stalin, both inside and out. I was surprised to find I hadn't completely forgotten the language. In fact, I not only understood everything people said; I found my ability to speak Russian came marvelously back to life.

The time my mother spent with me and those relaxing days in Moscow were very important to her. Her second husband had died some months earlier and she was still quite shaken. To make matters worse, my half-brother Aleksei had just started college. All at once, my mother felt alone and with nothing to look forward to. After twenty years of separation, I obviously had shown up at just the right moment. So I invited her to visit us in Brazil soon and spend a few months in hot Roraima during the harsh Russian winter. It would give her a wonderful chance to relax while getting to know her daughter-in-law Alice and her grandsons David and Benjamin.

Bulgaria, 1994

~~~~~~

After my stay in Moscow, I still had a few days left for a quick but emotional trip to Bulgaria, where things were complicated both politically and economically, and in the social sphere as well. When my Aeroflot flight landed in Sofia, I was surprised to find myself reacting as I had when I met my mother. "I'm getting old and soft," I said to myself. "Now I cry for any old reason."

When we had been approaching the city from the air, I had spotted Vitosha Mountain, iconic symbol of the city. I'd spent many hours on its slopes in my youth, hiking and skiing with friends on the weekends. When I was sixteen, I'd experienced my first crush, with a girl in my class, and it had started there too. The sight of the mountain woke so many memories, as if I were watching a movie of my life. The scenes continued flashing through my mind as my taxi headed to the Sheraton, in the heart of Sofia. It seemed like I'd been there only yesterday. There was Freedom Park and Eagles' Bridge; Sofia's trademark yellow pavement; St. Kliment Ohridski, also known as Sofia University; the monument to Russian Emperor Alexander II, who liberated Bulgaria from the Ottoman yoke in 1878; Alexander Nevsky Memorial Church; the palace; the somber Communist Party building; the huge ZUM department store; and St. Nedelya Church, the mosque, and the synagogue, the latter of which I'd never seen open. I was moved and at the same time startled—I realized downtown Sofia hadn't changed much in twenty years, except now the streets were potholed and dirty and the buildings were in very poor shape. It didn't take long for me to conclude that many people, who had never known things any other way, had yet to process the fall of the Communist regime.

The economy had formerly been bolstered by restrictive trade policies imposed on Eastern bloc nations by Moscow, rather than being grounded in efficiency or high-quality goods and services, and now it was a mess. The world market had no room for shabby, expensive goods, unlike Communism's protected markets. The transition to a market economy would clearly be difficult, and especially painful for the stunned senior citizens. It wouldn't be easy for young people either. An astounding 20% of the economically active population was jobless, the GDP had dropped 25% since the last year of the Communist regime, and the domestic outlook was bleak. The countless scientists, artists, engineers, doctors, and even philosophers who lacked steady employment eked out their living by doing odd jobs in manual labor, a humiliating experience for many. This triggered a mass exodus of Bulgarians to other countries. Unlike many other Europeans, the vast majority of the country's citizens had little experience importing or exporting human resources, and for them it seemed like the end of the world. It had only been during a brief period in the late nineteenth and early twentieth centuries that some Bulgarians had been bold enough to emigrate to countries like Canada, the United States, and Argentina. Emigration had been so uncommon among Bulgarians that they coined the term *"gurbet"* to describe the new phenomenon, where men left their families to earn money abroad for a few years, always with the intention of eventually returning. During the forty-five years of Communist rule, rigid controls had discouraged international travel and impeded the right to come and go, so there had been virtually no emigration. For other nations, emigration has always been a valid option. When their economies grew tight, Italians, Spaniards, Portuguese, Irish, Dutch, Polish, Scandinavians, Chinese, Indians, and even Germans and Japanese spread out across the world in pursuit of new opportunities, without this representing some kind of national tragedy. The result is evident in countries like the United States, Canada, Australia, South Africa, Argentina, and Brazil, where large communities of very diverse origins have colored the cultures of people in the New World. Hardly anyone knows that Giuseppe Garibaldi was a hero in Latin America before he ever became a national hero in his native Italy.

I didn't have any relatives left in Bulgaria and at first, I thought I probably wouldn't be able to track down my childhood friends. Things had changed so much. When I went to look my classmates up at their old addresses, nobody even remembered them. My last resort was an old friend of my father's, Plamen Varbanov, whose phone number I found in an old address book. To my surprise, the number still worked. Plamen was not only still alive—he remembered me as a child. He helped me locate some other childhood and college friends, so my three last days in Sofia were busy.

Only after I'd talked to Plamen and my friends did I begin to understand why—contrary to my expectations—the road from a rigid, unproductive Communist-style economy to a market one would be long and bumpy. Nobody knew quite what to do. The years of obedience and submission to the so-called "dictatorship of the proletariat" had dampened the entrepreneurial spirit and self-confidence of otherwise well-educated Bulgarians. And for good reason. Around the same time, I arrived, many of the new private banks were running into big trouble, and they nearly dragged the rest of the economy down the hole in the years that followed. In desperate times, charlatans will always come along dressed as saviors of the fatherland,

and it was no different in Bulgaria. The bewildered, unprepared people of Bulgaria fell easy prey to magic promises of fat, fast profits in the form of pyramid schemes. The results were disastrous for many and brought widespread economic collapse that year and for several more. And the State sank right along with its poverty-stricken citizens. To add pain to misery, those who had jobs saw runaway inflation slash their salaries to pitiful levels. Pensions plummeted to a ridiculous three dollars a month. On top of it all, I bore horrified witness to a veritable epidemic of unbridled crime during the short time I was there, including gunfire and murders in broad daylight, in a country that was clearly out of control. The government hadn't been so absent even in the prospecting region of Rondônia. It was sad to see.

I could never have imagined that right when this national tragedy struck, in the midst of chaos in the spring of 1994, Bulgarians would have their spirits raised so high that many proudly declared God to be Bulgarian, despite it all. It began in November 1993, when the country's national soccer team rose from the ashes in the 44th minute of the second half of a game in Paris, flipping the score to Bulgaria 2, France 1. A tie would have classified the host nation, but the unlikely transpired and the poor, impoverished nation of Bulgaria won a seed in that year's World Cup.

From that point on, the nation only grew more and more excited. It was amazing how this type of event could have such an impact on the spirit of a nation in profound crisis. And much else was yet to happen. No one even dreamed that the sports world would witness another miracle, at the world soccer championship in the United States. During those unforgettable days, divine grace was accompanied by the fierce, inspired playing of all the Bulgarian players, led by striker Stoichkov, who routed the giants Argentina and Germany to reach the quarter finals.

My week in Bulgaria was over in a flash. I barely had time to climb Vitosha and look down on the city from above. The crumbling facades and numerous potholes were invisible from afar, and the city looked much lovelier. I could see how the downtown had remained largely unchanged for twenty years, while much had grown up around it. The country would still have tough times ahead, but right then, standing on that scorched earth in 1994…for many people, God was truly Bulgarian.

The Children
of Santa Virginia

My mother's Lufthansa flight landed in Brazil on November 15, 1995, right on her birthday. After a brief rest in São Paulo, where I had to buy some new farm equipment, we headed up to Manaus. We stayed only a few days, long enough for Irina to meet her brother-in-law Licco and his family. Our visit was very short because I had to get back to the fazenda, where I had plenty of headaches to deal with. We didn't even stop in Boa Vista but, with Maria Bonita at the wheel of my pickup, took the highway straight from the airport to Santa Virgínia, on the banks of the Surumu River.

Alice was doubly happy to see the two women, especially Maria Bonita, who had come along as a surprise. They continued to share a tight mother-daughter bond, just as they had back in the rubber forests of Quatro Ases, lost in the jungle, and later in Porto Velho, where Alice had spent her childhood and early youth, in the company of her mother and brothers.

My mother fit in easily despite the language barrier. It was funny to watch the three women talk, mixing gestures, faces, words, mimicry, and even resorting to drawings to communicate as best they could. My mother's three-month visit flew by. It was wonderful to be with her again. It took a weight off me and relieved some of the guilt I felt about our long years apart.

I served as interpreter when we were all together, since I was the only one who spoke both Portuguese and Russian. The children spent the most time with the four women. David was five and Benjamin was still a toddler, just starting to say his first words. Conceição and Antônio's two little tow-haired girls were practically the same ages as our boys. David was a few months older than Taiana, and little Iara had been born less than a year before Benjamin. The children played together during the day, mostly in the company of their mothers, Alice and Conceição, and their grandmothers, Maria Bonita and Irina. The women were obviously enchanted with these happy, extroverted children and they loved pampering, protecting, and teaching them. It was too early to think about school, but since their formal education would eventually be a concern, we talked about it often. Up until the early 1980s, local farmers had sent their children to the Surumu Mission School. But then it became part of the Raposa Serra do Sol Indigenous Educational Center, subordinated to the Indigenous Council of Roraima, and it only accepted indigenous students. The alternatives would be to send them to school in Normandia; Boa Vista, the capital; or even out of state. It wouldn't be an easy decision.

Of the four children, only David had no Indian blood. Benjamin's indigenous features were strong and evident but, in contrast with his dark skin, he had hazel eyes with hints of green, gray, and yellow, coincidently the same shade as his adoptive mother's. Years earlier, when I'd met Alice and fallen in love with her, her eyes had reminded me of a wild ocelot. Although Alice and Benjamin had no blood ties, people often took them for mother and son, probably because of their eye color. Alice and I always made it clear to Benjamin that while he was our son and we loved him very much, just as we loved David, we were not his biological parents. We thought it would be better for him to learn this from us and not someone else.

He was too young for details, but it was important to think ahead and be truthful about it all. We've never regretted it, and I'm confident we took the right approach.

It was harder to detect the indigenous features in Antônio's daughters. The girls really stood out, with their ash-blond hair and green eyes, like their father's, which were unusual in that region. But their almond eyes and skin color—just a bit lighter in tone than the indigenous peoples—declared the presence of Indian blood, inherited from their Wapishana grandmother. From an early age, Taiana, the older girl, had displayed an uncanny ability to relate to the animals on the fazenda, first with Antônio's German shepherds and then with the horses. Antônio had something of this talent, but his daughter truly outdid him. At the age of four, she would accompany her father on his long rides through the *lavrado*, whenever he had the time. When the dogs got a thorn stuck in their paws (which was often), Taiana was in charge of extracting it. The animals would let her do things nobody else could get away with, not even Antônio, to whom they showed obedience in all else. This rare affinity eventually manifested itself with the horses as well. This wasn't altogether surprising, since Taiana spent hours with the animals, helping with clean-up and lovingly stroking them and combing out their manes and tails. Iara, the younger one, looked a lot like her sister, but the resemblance was only physical; their interests were different and Iara was quite introverted.

Once a year, almost always around the same time, herds of *lavradeiros* would come to the Surumu River region. We would always take our mares in heat and let them run free in the company of the wild horses for a few days. The *lavradeiros* were an attraction in and of themselves, and we loved watching them, even if only from afar. When I noticed their arrival that year, I decided to share the show with the children and their grandmothers. The women and children followed us on the dirt road in a small pickup, stopping a respectable distance away, where they could watch the herd without scaring the horses. Meanwhile, Antônio, little David and Taiana, and I cut across the fields on horseback. We picked a strategic location next to some huge termite mounds near the dirt road, so we could watch the herd.

"They'll be here a few more days. With any luck, we'll have some mares in heat and can set them loose in the herd," Antônio said. "I know this stud. He's a hot one!"

Right then I realized Taiana's mare had moved perilously close to the herd, apparently at the girl's direction. "Isn't that dangerous?" I asked in alarm.

"I don't know," Antônio replied, looking worried too. He cocked his gun, signaled for me to do the same, and motioned me to be quiet.

"I think the stud has spotted our mare. He must've seen Taiana too," Antônio whispered.

We were tense as the girl and her horse moved closer, only a few yards from the wild mares. But they remained calm and simply ignored her. None of the horses took off in a gallop. The male just whinnied a bit and stomped his hoof on the ground, but he didn't budge or exhibit any aggressive behavior. The tension drained from us when the mares went back to grazing. The small herd remained as peaceful as could be. For a few moments, Taiana had been right in the middle of the wild mares. So close that if she had reached out her arm, she could have touched their uncombed manes.

Then Antônio said in a voice so soft I could hardly hear him, "She went too far! Stay here. I'm going to go get her. I think the danger's gone but still, be ready to shoot."

Antônio moved in very slowly, making as little noise as possible. It wasn't long before the stud noticed him. It whinnied loudly, as if calling the herd's attention, and then took off in the opposite direction. The obedient females followed behind in a gallop, and Taiana was soon alone.

"Don't you ever pull that stunt again," Antônio chided her, at the same time exhibiting his relief.

Even though his voice told me how angry he was, I could also sense that Antônio was proud of his fearless little girl. After all, she'd managed to get incredibly close to the untamable *lavradeiros*. She was a true horse whisperer.

Another Bulgarian in the Amazon

Whenever things weren't real busy at the inn during the week, our two families, the Costas and the Hazans, usually ended the day with a lively dinner. The children played in one corner while we adults sat and chatted in the refreshing evening air, out on the farmhouse patio. One night, Antônio began reminiscing about another Bulgarian who had passed through the area many years earlier, a man by the name of Ilia Deleff. In 1933, Mário had made his first trip to the secret prospecting zone on the river, where he had mined a "hatful of diamonds." He'd used some of these diamonds to purchase Santa Virgínia Fazenda. His second venture to the same spot, in 1946, didn't bring him the same success, but he still made good money, enough for his family to enjoy relative prosperity for some time. Eleven years later, when Mário was sixty-three and Antônio was eleven, he needed money again. So father and son had set off on foot for what proved to be a three-week journey. Despite the rough terrain, they managed to reach the site at the headwaters of Arraia, a small branch of the upper Tacutu River. Along the way, Mário noticed how many things had changed over the preceding ten years—the most important being that many other people had discovered Mário's deposit and signs of prospecting activities were visible everywhere.

"The Arraia River wasn't all that wide, no more than a hundred to a hundred thirty feet across," Antônio said, choking up a bit as he remembered his childhood days. "The white-sand beaches on either side of the creek were covered with makeshift huts that had obviously been built in a hurry. We used a chunk of canvas and four poles to fashion a tent, and my father asked me to stay there and get to know our neighbors, while he took the lay of the land. He didn't come back for several hours, and when he finally did, I could tell he wasn't pleased. He sputtered something like 'This place is packed with people digging the river bottom up. I don't even recognize it anymore. We're going to leave tomorrow and look for another river and pray to God that He'll help us.'

"When the neighbors saw me, a hungry young boy, they were quick to offer food and so we ate our fill. There was plenty of game around there back then, so prospectors never went hungry. I was always amazed at the life they led in that crazy world. The prospectors lived extremely rough lives, whether they were mining for gold or diamonds. They worked under barbaric conditions. They were always fighting among themselves, and someone would occasionally be murdered. But at the same time, they were capable of showing compassion and kindness like you don't see even under much more civilized circumstances," Antônio said.

"I'm very familiar with all this," I broke in. "I witnessed that kind of camaraderie and support in Rondônia's mining fields. You don't very often see this type of generosity and concern for others in a big city."

Antônio went on with his story. "The next day, we told our neighbors goodbye and headed back down the Tacutu River. We walked down the beaches and sometimes cut through small stretches of forest. We were always exhausted by the end of the day, and we'd set up camp on a small, deserted beach. 'We'll sleep here tonight,' my dad said one night. 'We don't have any neighbors to help us today, but I've got a chunk of dried tapir leftover from yesterday.' I was puzzled and said, 'I didn't see you buy any meat, Dad. Where'd it come from?' Instead of answering my question, my father just smiled and said, 'Be grateful you've never gone hungry. Unfortunately, I've gone hungry a lot and that's why whenever I eat a meal, I always think about where my next meal is coming from.'

"Right then, a well-outfitted aluminum boat with a powerful motor, filled with prospecting gear, appeared out of nowhere and pulled up on the shore. Two men got out and one approached us. 'We're going to spend the night here,' he said. 'And don't worry—we're harmless.'

"The other fellow, who seemed to be the boss, set up a small tent in no time, while the first man put together a makeshift canvas shelter, like ours. Then they made a campfire. Some pickled fish even appeared on their improvised table. I think I know why the man who was evidently the owner of the boat came over and offered us some fish and flour, in broken Portuguese. My father was an older man with a young child, so he no doubt inspired trust. We ended up joining the two strangers for dinner, and our jerky was hidden away and saved for another day.

"They asked a lot of questions about the prospecting region up the river, and my father's descriptions clearly worried them. 'The place has given all it can. I did some prospecting there once and found a few diamonds. The only reason I didn't get more was that I was alone, and one man can't produce much. You need a team of three or four.'

"The boat owner seemed quite interested in what my father had to say. The two of them talked a long time and then we all went to sleep. It was so isolated there, you could hear the forest playing a concert of unimaginable sounds—the cries of parrots and macaws; sometimes a deep growl, like the quiet roar of a big cat. I was used to these sounds, but the foreigner wasn't. Before I dropped off to sleep, I saw him sitting on the riverbank, smoking and staring at the calm waters.

"The next day brought a pleasant surprise. When we were taking down our tent, the foreigner came over and started talking to my father in a mixture of Portuguese and Spanish. To make a long story short, he invited us to join his team. He offered us his boat, food, and tools; in exchange, my father would contribute his expertise on the region. It was a serious offer. The owner of the boat would keep half of whatever was produced, and his buddy and us would keep one-quarter each. A few minutes later, we all piled into the boat."

Antônio seemed to get immense pleasure out of recalling those days. After a brief silence, he went on: "Now comes the really surprising part. We knew the guy who owned the boat was named Ilia, and his friend was Arnaldo. We traveled down the Tacutu River, looking for a promising place to start testing. We tried a few branches that emptied into the main river but had no success. We used really crude methods to do our testing and prospecting. We'd put the mixture of gravel and sand from the river bottom into a kind of sieve with a diameter of twenty to twenty-four inches, and then we'd swirl it around in the water. Because of the relative weight of diamonds, they'd fall to the bottom of the sieve. Then, when we dumped it onto dry land, the precious metal would be on top, easy to spot and collect.

"At the end of the second day, we steered the boat into a short, shallow tributary. The mouth was narrow and shrouded with thick vegetation. It was hard to tell it apart from the main river. The sun had set, and we decided to spend the night on a small beach there. Testing would have to wait until the next day.

"Real early the next morning, while we were fixing breakfast right there where we'd camped out, my father was just messing around and ended up doing the first test. I'll never forget it! The first time he dumped his sieve, he started shouting, so we ran over to see what was up. We couldn't believe it: something was sparkling on top of the gravel, like an intense ray of light. It was a small, transparent, well-shaped octagonal crystal. Like a dream, I saw my father hug Ilia. I thought the two of them would start dancing. In his excitement, the foreigner shouted something. I think it must have been a curse word in his native language, which I didn't understand. But to my surprise, my father went nuts. You'd have thought a lightning bolt had hit the old man. He got all agitated and spoke to Ilia in a language that Arnaldo and I didn't recognize. Then it was Ilia's turn to be shocked.

"And that's how, as we collected our first diamond, two Bulgarians lost in the jungles of the Amazon met under utterly astonishing circumstances.

"By the end of the day, we'd found three more diamonds, one of them good sized, maybe four or five carats. 'This one's worth a mountain of money,' my father said, really thrilled.

"After such an extraordinary day, there was a lot of talking that night. The men opened a bottle of *cachaça* and the conversation flowed. I found out my father and Ilia were from the same country—the far-off, exotic Bulgaria, over in Europe. What's really a coincidence is that when they were young, my father and Ilia both worked as gardeners outside Bulgaria, although at different times and places—my father in Austria in the early twentieth century and Ilia in neighboring Czechoslovakia nearly fifty years later. It was easy to see that my father had a bit of trouble speaking that strange language after so many years without using it, and so the conversation continued in a mixture of Portuguese, Spanish, Bulgarian, and even German."

"How'd the guy end up in Roraima?" I asked.

"My father knew the story better than I do. I only remember that after traveling through a number of countries in South America, especially Venezuela, always with the dream of visiting the Amazon, Mr. Ilia Deleff—or *Bai* Ilia as my father called him—reached the Branco River Valley, via the Orinoco River, following in the footsteps of Alexander Humboldt, the German explorer who discovered the passage from the Orinoco Basin to the Branco River Basin, a passage that has never been thoroughly explored.

"We spent nearly a month at that hidden spot. We found a number of diamonds, ranging from small to medium, all of excellent quality. We got three hatfuls of the gems. But, unbelievable as it sounds, we never found another rock as big as the huge one we found the first day. Unfortunately, we committed a basic mistake that could easily have jeopardized all of our success. When we ran out of provisions, we went up the Tacutu River to the main prospecting area, where we sold the diamonds. I remember that my father's share came to over $80,000—a ton of money back then. The news raced through the region, and that's when we realized we should have gone straight to Boa Vista or maybe even Georgetown, without calling the attention of thousands of prospectors so close to where the diamonds lay. We couldn't get back to our spot anymore without being seen, because we were followed by boat day and night. As long as nobody else knew where we'd found our treasure, we were relatively safe.

"All the prospectors were waiting for us to return to our Eldorado for more of our bonanza. Everything would change if our deposit were discovered. We'd be targeted by the thieves who always hang around the mining areas. Everybody knew we had a lot of money, and plenty of guys in that pack of desperate prospectors had ulterior motives. My father, Arnaldo, and Ilia were armed but even so, we couldn't risk the slightest slip-up. Even if we didn't tell anyone where our deposit lay, we knew things would turn dangerous for us soon enough. You can recognize signs of prospecting activities, and it was only a matter of time before someone located our camp. We had to vanish before we became victims of violence. So one night, under cover of darkness, we filled the tank of our speedy boat and fled in the direction of Normandia, the city founded by the French prisoner from Devil's Island, Maurice Marcel Habert. We saw a few boats take off after us, but they couldn't catch up and soon gave up, because they didn't have enough fuel for a long pursuit. We reached Normandia two days later and continued straight on to Boa Vista, where we deposited the money in the bank. Deleff left not long after. He headed to Manaus and, unless I'm mistaken, traveled south to Minas Gerais. We went back to Santa Virgínia Fazenda.

"My father kept in touch with *Bai* Ilia until shortly before his death. He said that Ilia—he called him a visionary—invested all his prospecting earnings in a big collection of gigantic crystals, possibly the largest in the world. Back then, nobody thought those huge stones were worth much—some of them weighed a few tons. On one of the few occasions when he left Roraima, my father visited Ilia, who at that point was living Rio de Janeiro. He told me Ilia had sold part of his collection to a French museum and was now a very wealthy man; other museums around the world were after him for the rest of the collection, which was worth several million dollars. While my father was there, Ilia gave him a 'little diamond' as a present, one of those we had panned way back when. I still have it; I keep it with my father's documents. I don't know if *Bai* Ilia is still alive, or just how the story ended. He was certainly a different kind of fellow, and very generous. Dad said he donated an important part of his collection of giant crystals to his homeland of Bulgaria, which he had never for-gotten."

I was intrigued by this story of yet another Bulgarian in the Amazon. "This guy must be the most illustrious Bulgarian who ever came through here," I said. "You should try to track him down. Bulgarians apparently have a special liking for the state of Roraima—better put, for the Amazon. There are a good many Bulgarians living in the city of Manaus today. Most of them are musicians with the Philharmonic Orchestra. Even the renowned Sofia opera has performed at the Teatro Amazonas. Neither Marin Kostov, nor Ilia Deleff, nor my Uncle Licco Hazan, or much less me myself could ever imagine that one day…"

Demarcation

~~~~~~

Demarcation of the Raposa Serra do Sol reserve officially began in the 1970s, but it only gained momentum in 1996 under the administration of President Fernando Henrique Cardoso. The government's initial proposal allowed those impacted by demarcation to contest it; the idea would be to exclude rural lands from the indigenous area if title had been held for many years, an approach known as discontinuous demarcation. The first party to feel wronged by this milder approach to creating the reserve, and the first to contest it, was the Roraima state government—heading a long list of other petitioners. For a brief time, it appeared the matter would be settled peacefully with the help of the state, and in the form of a compromise acceptable to all sides.

What ensued was a series of legal battles and lawsuits. The original understanding was that property would be excluded if the owner's deed predated the Constitution of 1934 or if the courts had previously handed down a final ruling in a land dispute, but such cases accounted for barely 2% of the total land in question. This idea gradually fell by the wayside under pressure from countless NGOs, foreign governments, the Catholic Church, and federal institutions and bodies, like FUNAI, the agency in charge of indigenous affairs. This despite the fact that some of the Indians themselves, the Brazilian Army, the State of Roraima, and rice producers and other farmers disagreed.

Antônio and I watched with growing concern as the disputes gradually progressed into violence. Cattle theft became common; fences and electric towers were toppled, and bridges quite literally burned. Word among the farmers—now deemed intruders or violent invaders—was that one farm alone had lost 3,000 head of cattle, along with fencing and other facilities. Earlier, Brazil's Supreme Court had recognized this same farm as private property belonging to a family of settlers, but it nevertheless became part of demarcated land. Under the rules in force up to that point, the courts were not supposed to decide against vested rights, *res judicata*, or any other matter adjudged— principles that still held in those parts of Brazil lying south of the equator. Of course, this change in the rules only added fuel to the fire, on both sides, among those who favored continuous demarcation and those who were against it (often times Indians belonging to one same tribe).

In December 1998, Justice Minister Renan Calheiros signed a ruling that declared Raposa Serra do Sol a single, unbroken indigenous territory. Up until then, both of our families had bravely remained in Santa Virgínia, but we couldn't delay our departure any longer. On the one hand, our children needed to go in school; at the same time, the government's decision would no doubt trigger even more radical reactions. The conflict had always been less violent around Santa Virgínia Fazenda. In part, this was because of our friendship with *tuxaua* Genival, but there had been unmistakable signs that his leadership was hotly contested inside his own community. In early 1999, one month after the federal government's decision, my family moved to Manaus; around the same time, the Costas moved to Boa Vista. I have a clear memory of our last act before leaving the fazenda: we buried Sharo, our furry friend and protector, who died of old age. In his final months, he'd gone completely blind and could hardly move. We all suffered with him and felt like we'd lost a family member. It hit Antônio and Taiana hardest; they had a remarkable tie to that amazing animal. We named a new

Sharo, a dog that had already been leading the rest of the pack for a while.

Even after we moved to Manaus, Antônio and I still spent a lot of time on the fazenda because we were now partners in our rice growing operations. The inn was going strong, as were the crops. Genival would stop by Santa Virgínia at least once a month, sometimes arriving by dugout, sometimes on horseback, and sometimes, more recently, on the back of his son Moacir's motorcycle. He'd often stay at the inn overnight, sleeping in a hammock outside since he didn't like to be cooped up inside four walls. On those occasions, he'd always ask about the women and children, who only visited the fazenda in January, during summer vacation. Antônio's family lived much closer, in Boa Vista, so they came more often. The girls were used to life on the farm; they really loved it and didn't like living in a cramped house behind high fences in the city. I spent more and more time with my own family in Manaus, and we only went back to the farm together during the children's summer vacation. Antônio gradually took on a bigger role in the rice business.

It was apparent that whenever the families were around, *tuxaua* Genival spent more time than usual chatting with everyone. He clearly enjoyed talking with Alice, to whom he had entrusted baby Benjamin years ago, and it was obvious how much he liked the Costa family and especially their daughter Taiana. The Indians who worked on the farm spoke among themselves about the young girl's uncanny ability to talk to the wild horses. Whenever the topic came up, the *tuxaua* paid especially close attention. Ever since Taiana was little, she had loved to watch the wild horses run loose across the *lavrado*; she'd stare at them from afar for hours. One day Genival happened to notice a herd going by and followed from a distance. Much to the old *tuxaua*'s surprise, twelve-year-old Taiana was riding among them. Most astoundingly, the horses seemed totally comfortable with her there. When the herd stopped, she fearlessly dismounted and went from wild mare to wild mare, stroking their long manes, which danced in the wind. The scene brought back sweet memories from the old Indian's childhood, when he had often watched in secret as another young girl, Iolanda, member of the Wapishana nation, moved among the skittish animals, petting their hides.

What nobody had ever figured out was that Genival, then a teenager but already the tribe's future leader, had fallen in love with a beautiful girl from another village, who married the farmer Mário Costa not long after that. Antônio was born less than a year later. Much to everyone's despair, it was a complicated delivery. The lovely Wapishana girl lost a great deal of blood and then developed a generalized infection, to which she eventually succumbed. Stunned and heartbroken, Mário never fully recovered. For many years afterward, he would visit his beloved wife's grave at the end of each day. She was buried not far from the main farmhouse, on an embankment from where he could gaze out at the Surumu River and beach. The servants swore they could hear him engaged in long conversations with Iolanda, as if she could hear him. He never remarried, but devoted his whole life to Santa Virgínia and his son, fruit of a love interrupted too soon. Mário's friendship with Genival dated to those days, when Antônio was still just a child.

Nobody, child or adult, had had such a close relationship with the wild horses since Iolanda's time. But now, so many years later, it seemed like the Wapishana girl had been reborn in her granddaughter.

The *tuxaua* was especially fond of Benjamin of course, since he had saved the boy from certain death years earlier and entrusted him to Alice's care. Genival was still a strapping man, but he was old. He stopped by shortly after the family arrived at the fazenda in January 2004. It was obvious how much his health had declined over the previous year. His trademark energy had drained away; instead, he seemed weak and had trouble walking. He asked to see Benjamin right away. The boy had grown a lot over the previous year and was quite tall for his age. Genival was shocked at how big he was. With one hand on Benjamin's arm, the *tuxaua* called Alice and me to one side and said, "It's time for Genival to tell you a secret."

He turned to the Indian who had accompanied him and said, "Bring the boy."

Minutes later, the other man returned with a young Indian who had clearly dressed up for the occasion. His large straw hat covered so much of his face that we couldn't get a good look at him.

"Take off your hat," the *tuxaua* ordered. The boy obeyed, revealing a face bronzed by the sun.

"My God!" Alice exclaimed. "He looks just like Ben-ja-min!"

Benjamin was staring at the other boy with a mixture of surprise and curiosity. The Indian boy was thinner and quite a bit shorter than he was, but the two of them looked so much alike.

"This is my grandson Fernando, my daughter Janaína's boy," the *tuxaua* explained. "She had twins and couldn't take care of them both. Dona Alice, your son is my grandson. One day, he and Fernando will be very important to our people and to Raposa. They must be friends." We could tell the *tuxaua* was very happy. "Fernando was bigger and stronger back then. Now Benjamin is."

Genival's emotions had gotten the better of him and he paused to regain his composure. We invited them all to have something to drink with us at the inn's restaurant. The boys needed time to get to know each other. I'll never forget the sight of the twin brothers that day, riding their bikes in the farmyard, the other children behind them, wondering at the resemblance. We left the twins to their games. We could hear their happy voices and spontaneous laughter, the kind of laughter only young, innocent children can enjoy.

A little while later, the laughter stopped, and the children came over to us.

"Fernando left," David said. "His father came and took him off on his motorcycle."

"That's Gerônimo, his step-father," Genival said, visibly displeased. "He doesn't like you folks."

So that memorable afternoon came to an early end.

It was the last time we saw *tuxaua* Genival.

The Beginning
of the Final Battle

January 2004, the height of summer vacation, was a busy time for the residents of Raposa Serra do Sol. Under the leadership of Paulo César Quartiero, a rice producer and influential politician, a number of other rice growers, as well as Indians who were in favor of discontinuous demarcation and preservation of the rice production areas and Lake Caracaranã, invaded the FUNAI headquarters in Boa Vista and closed roads and bridges. The farmers were desperate. The most obvious example of this was the destruction of the historic building at Surumu Mission, which housed the offices of the Raposa Serra do Sol Center for Indigenous Training and Culture. As part of what was a dirty little game, facts were twisted and blame thrown on the victims, who were accused of setting fire to their own facility.

This wouldn't get anyone anywhere. The Brazilian government had already made its political decision, and the only thing left was for the courts to deliver their formal ruling.

On April 15, 2005, President Luiz Inácio Lula da Silva signed a decree enacting continuous demarcation—in other words, the new indigenous reserves would include lands legally held by private landowners, land that had sometimes been in the same family for generations. The state governor was extremely upset and declared a week of official mourning. The Federal Police then launched Operation Upatakon, which would remove non-Indians from the region. It was useless for farmers to show their deeds or titles or point out that the Macuxis, who came from the Caribbean, had been invaders just as much as the settlers who had lived there since receiving title from the Brazilian Empire in 1877. Four generations later, the incredulous descendants of these settlers found themselves on the verge of being kicked off land that the Brazilian State itself had handed over to their grandparents years earlier.

There were plenty of other violent reactions during the months and years following signature of the decree. Highways were closed and vital bridges destroyed, with both sides engaging in acts of vandalism. Settlers felt their own defeat was imminent, and their frustration only grew when the government announced how much they would pay for the land—values well below the market.

Things were so tense that an outright confrontation seemed inevitable, with rice growers and other settlers openly threatening to resist. Even Antônio surprised me one day, showing me a veritable arsenal of heavy weapons and ammunition carefully hidden in the basement of his home.

"It won't be for a shortage of weapons! I'm not going to just hand over on a silver platter the land where my parents are buried, where I was born and raised, and where my daughters were born! Paulo César must have a lot more weapons and he's determined to resist. All the rice growers are arming themselves and there are other farmers and many Indians who'll support us."

"Emotions are running so high that we're pretty close to an unprecedented bloodbath," I said. I was extremely worried.

"Are you going to help? We're going to need people like you, people who have experience in armed resistance. Prospectors coming in from Rondônia still remember you. Sounds like you really got into things up there and know your way around a good fight. In fact, you said you were in the Israeli Army." As usual, Antônio cut right to the chase.

I wasted no time telling him I wouldn't take part in any violence and was hoping for a peaceful solution. Even though I understood his indignation and outrage, I told him it would be foolhardy to risk our lives, and many other people's, for a lost cause.

"Well, there's one hope left. The Supreme Court is going to rule on the matter."

For the thousandth time, Antônio went on and on about the region's history. He was furious that nobody seemed to be taking into account the fact that this part of the world belongs to Brazil and not Guyana only because migrants from the Brazilian Northeast had settled in the region of the Maú River in the second half of the nineteenth century, establishing immense cattle ranches there. When Brazil and England disputed those lands in the early twentieth century, the Brazilian statesman Joaquim Nabuco managed to solve the conflict through international arbitration. Thanks to the resilience of those pioneers, who without any government help confronted all sorts of danger and hardships, Brazil had a heavy presence in the area. In 1904, Italy's King Victor Emmanuel III, the arbiter, gave Brazil all the territory west of the Maú River, where Raposa Serra do Sol now lies. Brazil never extended any form of recognition to the anonymous heroes who won this land for their country. And if that weren't enough, now, precisely 100 years later, their grandchildren were being unceremoniously and unapologetically kicked off their land.

"Are the judges in Brasilia fully aware of the history of these lands?" Antônio didn't sound very hopeful when he posed this question.

My friend and I were sitting on the farmhouse patio. The inn was still drawing a few guests, but the discouraging events had really slowed business down lately. Our families were far away, and the empty house didn't hold the happiness it had in the past.

I knew if I didn't change the subject, Antônio would talk about this all night, so I broke in. "There's a part of Raposa I've never been to: the city of Uiramutã, way up north. You know the region better than I do, so I imagine you know how long it takes to get there."

"I haven't been to Uiramutã in a while," he said. "I don't know what kind of shape highway RR-171 is in, or whether all the bridges are open, but I think it would be an eight-hour drive from Normandia, tops."

"Maybe I could head up there next weekend. I've heard it's lovely there in the mountains, with lots of waterfalls around." I was really interested in making the trip. "I could go up one day and come back the next."

"I'll go with you. It'd be worth the drive. It really is lovely up there. Let's take off Friday morning and come back Sunday afternoon," Antônio said.

Uiramutã

State highway RR-433 was in good shape. It was the dry season, and this helped the drive. The narrow wooden bridges seemed to be just fine, even though there were never any side rails. Highway RR-171 got really bad toward the end, with lots of upgrades and downgrades and plenty of mud holes, but our 4-wheel drive pickup met the challenge. As planned, we were in Uiramutã by early afternoon. It was a small town with a population of less than five thousand.

"Let's find somewhere to spend the night and then grab some food," said Antônio.

A small billboard on the outskirts of town announced an inn, which was located one block down the main street. The entrance to the small one-story building opened onto a crowded dining hall, where half a dozen indigenous women were eating some peculiar mishmash. It didn't look very good, and my first impression was that the place wasn't very clean. An elderly gentleman came over and introduced himself.

"Coronel Romualdo, owner of Pick and Pay Inn."

I was so busy being underwhelmed by the place that I didn't quite catch what he said.

"Fish and Pay?" I asked. "There's no water here. Where are the fish?"

When the so-called colonel chuckled, I noticed he had hardly any teeth. "Well, the 'little fishies' are nibbling on some food right now. They're sitting over there, waiting for customers. We don't have any rooms right now, but we will in an hour or two."

This wasn't at all what we had in mind, so we hurried out. It didn't take us long to find another little hotel, much nicer and cleaner, with the encouraging name Sunny Inn. We got the last vacancy. The other guests were prospectors, almost all in the company of local girls—no surprise, considering it was the weekend—and the place was much more inviting than the foreboding Pick and Pay. The beds were nothing more than wooden frames with a sheet thrown over them to serve as a mattress, but the room was clean and there was a bathroom. We left our things and went out to take a walk around the small town. We learned it was the site of an important Special Border Platoon of the Brazilian Army and that the economy revolved around the region's prospectors. It all reminded me of the mining area in Rondônia. The only big difference was that ore was extracted from fields here, not rivers. It was easy to spot the damage caused by mining activities near the town, and I realized that much greater invisible damage must have been caused by the mercury that poisons the environment. And in such a beautiful place.

It had been a long day. Right after sunset, we grabbed a bland pizza at the first diner we stumbled on. Then we went back to the inn and got ready to spend the night in our uncomfortable beds. We planned to get up early the next morning to check out the waterfalls in the surrounding area, but what we weren't counting on was the cold that hit in the middle of the night. It was particularly hard to take it because we didn't have any blankets, and the light clothing we wore during the day didn't do any good warming us up either. The town was nestled in the mountain region of Raposa Serra do Sol, where the temperature varies from sizzling hot during the day to frigid cold at night. It was the middle of the night and there was nobody at the front desk, so we used the hotel's small bath towels to cover up as best we could. We were shivering so hard we couldn't fall back to sleep, so the solution was to talk a while.

"Oleg, what would you do in my position, with what we're going through in Raposa?" I could tell the question had been stuck in Antônio's throat.

I'd already answered a dozen similar questions over the course of that day. This time I paused a while before saying anything. I decided I wouldn't sugar-coat things for my friend. "In your place, I'd get ready to vacate my paradise. From what I understand, you'll be compensated only for the buildings and improvements but not for the land, which, after all, is your biggest asset. Before it's too late, sell any irrigation equipment you have, sell those useless guns and the cattle you've still got, and don't invest a penny more until a final ruling has been handed down. Like my cousin the judge always says, 'justice may delay, but it doesn't fail.'"

"It's painful. Because this time, it looks like justice will fail," Antônio muttered.

"Let's keep hoping. Maybe the Supreme Court will decide in our favor. There are plenty of reasons for it." I had to be frank, while still consoling my friend.

"Unfortunately, there are anthropological and legal reasons for ruling against us too. The tendency today is to consider the Indians as the rightful land owners—the only owners." Antônio was being a true realist. "For years, they were killed off with the blessings of the government, the public at large, the courts, and even the church. So now all these institutions are viewing the current fight as the only opportunity for righting these wrongs. Just imagine how the politicians, bureaucrats, clerics, and even judges are going to fill themselves with pride for being so 'humanitarian'. And we'll pay the price. There are so few of us that they can simply ignore us."

"That's what I'm afraid of," I agreed. "There's an irresistible temptation to hand down an insubstantial, populist ruling. Nobody is even going to remember that it was the settlers who conquered this part of the world for Brazil early last century. Everyone knows full well there was virtually no Brazilian government in the region during the lopsided conflict with mighty England, and at no point did the international arbiters take the Indians into consideration. Without the heavy presence of the tough men from the Northeast, the *lavrado* would belong to British Guiana today."

It was early morning before sleep overtook us. The sun quickly began warming things up.

Sunny Inn put on a good breakfast, and that's precisely what Antônio and I needed after a poor supper and sleepless night. We had just started eating when we heard a woman exclaim: "My God! Oleg! Here at my inn!"

A heavy-set middle-aged woman, who had been tidying up the dining room, had evidently recognized me from somewhere. I hadn't expected to run into anyone the first time I set foot in that remote corner of the world.

"Do I know you, ma'am?" I didn't really have much interest in the answer.

"The last time I saw you was in Palmeiral, at Sandra Reis's nightclub. I was a young girl and worked for her. My artistic name was Niara. It's been twenty years. You probably don't remember me."

I couldn't believe my ears. I took a closer look at the woman, and an image flashed into my mind of a very pretty, thin young girl with an hourglass figure and a salty sway in her broad hips. She had been the brightest star at the Casa da Lola brothel, located on the Madeira River in far-off Rondônia, in the prospecting region. Niara Nutbuster! Who hadn't heard of that insatiable firebrand—the hottest woman in the mining region for years? The change was unbelievable. Now she was a plump, congenial middle-aged woman who looked like a quiet housewife.

"Dona Sandra treated you like a son. We weren't even allowed to talk to you. I was always a fan of yours, even more after the War of Prainha. Welcome to Uiramutã and my home. And by the way," she said quietly, "my real name is Isabel."

I introduced Antônio, and the three of us struck up a good conversation. Isabel told me she was married to a former prospector, Laureano, nicknamed Baiano, who had owned a dredge. They had two children. He wasn't in Uiramutã but would be coming back from Boa Vista some time that day.

"I take care of the inn. Laureano has the best overseer in me, his wife, and he can travel without any worries," Isabel said with a good dose of pride. "Please say you'll join us for dinner tonight, after your day out. My husband knows you, and he'll be very honored to have you here, Russo. You might remember him. He was a regular client at Casa da Lola."

It was clear she remembered me well after all those years—right down to my nom de guerre. We were happy to accept her invitation.

Before saying goodbye, Isabel lowered her voice and said, "But please don't call me by my artistic name. Laureano doesn't like it." And she moved away with a discrete sway of her hips, just like in the old days.

"Antônio, Isabel likes you," I teased my friend. "She's no doubt a faithful, devoted wife now, but you don't know what a hit she was twenty years ago, really popular. Word was that Niara Nutbuster couldn't stand to have an erect cock near her. She'd take care of it immediately, leaving it limp and broken. Ergo her name."

We had a great day. There wasn't much for tourists to see in the small town, and the food at the local diners wasn't very tasty, but the nearby mountains were breathtakingly beautiful. Uiramutã actually had a bit of everything to offer: mountains, tropical rainforests, savannahs, rivers, and shaded waterfalls that spilled into calm natural pools with clear, inviting waters.

I remembered that Uiramutã would probably lie outside the future reserve and I thought it would be fun to come back with Alice and the children. They'd love the trip. It also occurred to me that Maria Bonita and Roberto would probably enjoy seeing Niara too. Maria had been the cook at Casa da Lola for years, before she worked on my dredge, and she knew the famous Niara very well. Just running into her had made our trip worth it.

"And we're going to have dinner here tonight. I'm sure it's going to be better than last night's pizza," Antônio said with a big grin.

When we got back to the hotel later, we had our first surprise of the night—our things had been moved to another room, much bigger and more comfortable. More importantly, the beds had been made up with comfortable mattresses and blankets.

"We've been saved," I said cheerfully. "We're going to sleep well tonight, and I'm giving you fair warning: I won't answer any of your questions after midnight."

At dinner, I recognized Isabel's husband immediately. I'd sold him more than one outboard motor back when I'd worked at Berimex.

"Welcome, Russo! It's an honor for us to receive such illustrious guests at our hotel," Laureano said with obvious satisfaction.

We didn't run out of subjects to talk about that night. We ate in the back of the hotel, where the family had a cozy home. Although Laureano was known as Baiano, he actually wasn't from the state of Bahia but from the far southern state of Rio Grande do Sul, so the food was of course a typical *gaúcho* barbecue. What Antônio and I hadn't eaten on our first night in Uiramutã, we made up for at this dinner. It ended with everyone enjoying a traditional *chimarrão*—yerba mate drunk piping hot out of a gourd.

Laureano had stayed in Palmeiral until the prospecting boom ended there in 1990, so he knew a lot that I didn't. "Your buddies, Cabeção and Chico Paraíba, were among the last to leave," he told me, referring to two owners of gold dredges who had been with me during the War of Prainha. "Their stubbornness cost them a lot of money. With the little they had, they recently tried their luck at Ji-Paraná, where they run a gas station now."

"Amorim, the one who had the outboard motor repair shop, died some years ago," Laureano went on.

"I heard about him," I said. "His son, Roberto, married Maria Bonita, my mother-in-law."

Now it was Baiano's turn to be surprised. "I didn't know you were related. Back then, Maria Bonita lived up to her name—she was the prettiest gal in the prospecting region. Next to Isabel, of course."

"We weren't relatives then," I explained. "Dona Sandra relinquished Maria Bonita to me, and she worked nearly two years on my dredge. Then I met her daughter, Alice. We got married and have two children."

"Maria Bonita's daughter must be lovely, and a great cook," Laureano said.

I didn't reply. There was no point explaining that my wife didn't share any of Maria Bonita's genes. And even so, she was indeed lovely and an excellent cook.

"Maria Bonita and Roberto live in Boa Vista, where he's a professor. I'll bring them with me next time I come to Uiramutã, and it won't be long," I promised.

Not unexpectedly, talk soon turned to a matter vital to us all, Raposa Serra do Sol. Laureano listened to Antônio's story and then said: "I've got a place that's being expropriated too. It's not as big as yours, but until a little while ago, we had over a thousand head. Despite my complaints, I lost over three hundred. The Indians just carried them off. I reported it a bunch of times, but the police didn't do a thing. I couldn't take it anymore, so I sold all the animals I had left. We still have a nice house there, along with our other improvements to the land. I think the land reform agency is assessing it. I don't know what value they're going to put on it, but I don't have great hopes. The compensations don't usually cover even a third of the investments. We're actually being evicted before final demarcation. The Court hasn't delivered its verdict yet, but honestly, we're no longer viewed as upstanding citizens."

Before dinner was over, Isabel insisted on taking me to see her children, who were already asleep in their beds.

"They're adorable! God bless them. They're the same age as my boys," I said, thinking fondly of David and Benjamin.

We were alone in the room, but Isabel lowered her voice so much that it was hard for me to hear her. "When I look at them, I know I've made it, praise God. But my poor friend Mocha Louca, she died of that terrible disease there's no cure for. It's all about luck."

"It's all about luck." I repeated. "Luck—and at least some degree of merit."

〰〰〰〰〰〰〰〰〰〰〰〰〰〰〰〰〰

We returned from Uiramutã the next day. As soon as we pulled into the farmyard, we realized something must have happened while we were gone. Instead of the usual warm welcome from our furry friend Sharo, we were met by a veritable delegation of farm workers, some carrying guns. As I stepped out of the truck, I noticed a pile of charred wood in a corner of the yard; some of it was just ashes.

"Part of our fence," explained the foreman of the rice fields. "The Indians set fire the day you left."

"What about Genival?" I asked.

"Genival died last Thursday at a hospital in Boa Vista. FUNAI took him there when he got sick, early last week. The tribe has already elected a new *tuxaua*. They chose that Gerônimo fellow, the one who lives with Genival's daughter, Janaína. That's only made things worse. He's anything but our friend. So they tried to burn down the fence."

"What about Sharo?" We could see some other German shepherds in the yard, but Antônio's companion wasn't among them.

"He took an arrow. Nobody saw it happen, but we think he went after the Indians when they were setting fire to the fence. He was dead when we found him."

Antônio looked like he had taken the arrow himself. I could tell he was so upset that he might lose control. It was no time for pity but for offering a helping hand and some thoughtful advice. With Genival's death, open conflict had come to Santa Virgínia.

Antônio and I had shared many close moments over the years, and I'd come to appreciate his fine qualities as a friend, business partner, father, and skilled manager. Now that we were moving into the final stretch of the battle over Raposa Serra do Sol, and ever closer to losing Santa Virgínia Fazenda, he surprised me by demonstrating another quality, and it made me admire him even more: the ability to experience adversity, and understand and acknowledge opinions different from his. On more than one occasion, I witnessed him talking things over with representatives of the Indigenous Council of Roraima while showing no signs of irritation, temper, or arrogance.

The day after we returned from Uiramutã, we went to have a frank talk with Gerônimo, before a bigger tragedy could strike. First, we sent a cousin of his who worked on the farm to let him know we were going to visit the village, unarmed and on a peace mission.

We let the other side have a few hours to get organized and then, accompanied by some of the Indians who worked at the inn, went over to the village. We stopped in a large clearing just short of the village itself, so they'd see us there. We stood waiting quite a while. It was clear they weren't happy about our visit and that we weren't welcome. After we'd waited nearly an hour, Gerônimo showed up with my son Benjamin's brother Fernando and some other Indians. While they weren't acting especially friendly, it was a good sign that they were also un-armed. We waited for Gerônimo to start talking first. His Por-tuguese was remarkably fluent.

Speaking in a firm voice, Gerônimo said he had nothing to do with the previous week's events and assured us it wouldn't happen again. We breathed a sigh of relief. The *tuxaua* made it clear that the Indigenous Council of Roraima had pledged to the Brazilian authorities that they wouldn't engage in any vio-lence while the courts were ruling on the matter, but there was no room for friendship with us.

I looked at Fernando. I could tell he was avoiding my eyes.

I admit I was quite nervous and worried Antônio might do something rash, but he limited himself to expressing our sym-pathy for Genival's passing and ended the conversation there. I don't know if I could have remained as calm and even-tem-pered in the same situation.

The Bitter End

In June 2007, Brazil's Supreme Court handed down a ruling evicting non-Indians from Raposa Serra do Sol. In March 2008, the Federal Police launched the last phase of Operation Upatakon and forcibly removed anyone who was still resisting the legal decision. It was a war scene. There were Federal Police squad cars and agents all over, armed to the teeth. The Roraima state government reacted by lodging a petition to contest the eviction order, based on the argument that it ran counter to the interests of the majority of the state's residents. The conflict led to fatalities on both sides, so the operation was suspended once again, until final rulings could be handed down on all pending legal matters related to the reserve.

On March 19, 2009, following a series of arguments for and against, Brazil's Supreme Court confirmed demarcation of Raposa Serra do Sol in a single, continuous territory. It was a historical ruling. April 30, 2009 was set as the deadline for the departure of any non-Indians. Just as Antônio Costa had feared, the game was coming to an end, and it was nothing less than humiliating. As expected, the winners and even some of the judges were jubilant: "Based on our ruling, Brazil can now look into the mirror of history without blushing in shame. With this ruling, Brazil has restored its dignity, by treating Brazilian Indians as our beloved brothers," declared one eminent Supreme Court justice.

I was in Manaus when the first justices announced their opinions. They all ruled in favor of continuous demarcation of the reserve and the immediate eviction of the "invaders"—

which is how the rice growers and other farmers were now labeled. I had to talk to Antônio right away. I knew he must be devastated. I was concerned my friend might do something reckless.

Technological progress had greatly facilitated life in Roraima's *lavrado* in recent years. There were now plenty of ways to communicate, something that hadn't been the case until quite recently. Satellite dishes transmitted the full range of Brazilian television channels and, for good or bad, kept the entire immense country of Brazil talking about the same things: soap operas, soccer games, and political passions. Satellite phones, and especially radio phones, had been another revolution, bringing national and international news to the most remote corners of the Amazon in real time. Like everywhere else around the world, the latest quotations from the Chicago Stock Exchange were a normal topic of conversation, even among farmers on far-off rivers in the Amazon. I knew that wherever Antônio was, he'd be following the voting in Brasilia and be aware of imminent defeat. For him and his family, it was the end of the world. I tried calling his radio phone and his landline in Boa Vista and even tried Conceição's cell, but nobody answered. I wanted to express my support, because my friend was about to lose nearly everything, he and his family had built over eighty years and two generations. I kept trying throughout the day, but nobody picked up anywhere. That night, the radio phone finally came to life and I heard my friend's familiar voice.

"I've been following the Court's voting," Antônio told me, soundly oddly calm. "Our loss was expected, but I was surprised the ruling was unanimous. Well, unanimity is always stupid, as Nelson Rodrigues said. Considering how controversial this matter has been, I think it's very odd that all eight justices who have ruled so far did so in favor of continuous demarcation. And remember, a number of justices on this same court recognized the validity of certain land deeds earlier. There must've been a lot more pressure on them this time."

I agreed. "I can't understand some of the justices, who argued that the people who bought land in the region of the intended indigenous reserve—and with the backing of the Brazilian government back then—hadn't really bought anything and therefore have no rights. In blunt terms, this is nothing but double talk."

"A lot of questions are still unanswered," Antônio said. "How can they say government-issued deeds are now worthless? When eminent domain is used, why is the compensation so low, and not at market value? Some justices haven't handed down their opinions yet, but I don't hold out hope." He seemed calm, but I could tell how upset he was.

"Get off the reserve as fast as you can. Don't wait any longer." I was adamant. "The game's over. The broad public is going to think the justices have presented perfectly sound arguments, because people don't know the full story and don't feel this loss personally. I see no chance for a reversal. A lot of the rice growers and other farmers are arguing that it's a question of malfeasance, but I don't think so. The justices seem to naively believe they're handing down justice. But the truth is, a number of historical facts—facts most people just don't know about—weren't taken into account."

"I'm at the farm with Conceição and the girls," Antônio said. "We've been keeping an eye on the news all day, and that's why I didn't pick up. My daughters can't comprehend what's happening. After all, they were born here. The land belonged to their grandparents, who are buried here. Now they've been labeled invaders and have to leave their home at gunpoint. I'd like to find a judge who could come here and explain this ruling to these children. I sure can't." He was irate.

"It'll take a while before it hits your daughters. What matters now is getting your family's life back together," I countered. "I'll try to help you as much as I can."

"I'm going to take the girls out for a drive around the *lavrado* tomorrow. Right now, I can't think any farther ahead than that," Antônio said in a dejected voice. "I've got forty days to get everything off the farm. I've already sold some of the cattle. The Indians took the rest. I've still got about forty head of Nelore, plus the horses and German shepherds."

"Just one more thing: Be careful. Try to avoid any friction with the Indians from here on in. Don't even go near Genival's village," I advised. "I'll fly into Boa Vista next week, and we can talk more. I'll stay at Hotel Aipana. I've got a few free days and can help you move off the farm. Maybe Alice will want to join me. But don't say anything to anyone until I can confirm the dates."

Antônio liked the idea. "We can drive up to Santa Virgínia and get all the cattle out," I continued. "I'll invite Roberto and Maria Bonita to come along."

We said goodbye, because there was nothing else to say.

Our Last Goodbye

~~~~~~

When I told Antônio our trip to Boa Vista was on and that Alice and the boys would be coming too, he was thrilled. "Let's surprise Conceição," he suggested. "She really misses you all and she'll love it."

Two days later, Antônio called to confirm everything. We decided we'd also surprise Maria Bonita with my family's visit. With Maria's help, Conceição would give a dinner party for me and her husband's other guests at their home in Boa Vista. Then, as the big surprise, David, Benjamin, and Alice would suddenly appear. It was also decided that we'd spend the week at Fazenda Santa Virgínia. We'd leave on Monday, hauling back the rest of the cattle and the bulk of the Costa family's belongings.

We landed around noon on Thursday and went straight to Hotel Aipana, conveniently located on the town's main square. Antônio and Roberto got to the hotel in the late afternoon, each in his own car. We had a beer by the pool and split into two groups: Antônio and me, and Roberto with the rest of my family. We all got to the Costas's home in the neighborhood of Paraviana around the same time.

Antônio and I went right in. I gave Conceição and Maria each a big hug, and we started catching up on the news. Everything seemed normal. Antônio called us out onto the porch to show us the beautiful *tambaqui* they were making for dinner. I remarked on the size of the fish. We tried to act as nonchalant as possible. But when we went back into the living room, Alice,

David, and Benjamin were sitting around the table—as if nothing unusual had happened and they'd been there for hours. Only then did Maria Bonita and Conceição realize they'd been duped. Even though we were going through a rough time, about to lose Santa Virgínia Fazenda forever, we could still enjoy being together like old times. The room was filled with laughter.

Conceição admitted that she had found it odd when Antônio told her he had invited three unknown guests on the same night they were receiving us, but she hadn't questioned her husband. Those days, there were plenty of reasons to meet with other farmers who were in the same boat and talk over possible joint actions.

Antônio was going to need help moving his cattle and horses, as well as his irrigation equipment and harvesters. Many Indians were already celebrating their victory and didn't hide the fact that they were impatient with the farmers still inside the reserve. Despite the massive presence of the Federal Police, there was a risk of violence breaking out and that could make the slow transportation of heavy equipment especially perilous. Transporting the animals would be even riskier since the Indians weren't at all happy about their removal. There were rumors that they'd taken hundreds of head of cattle in recent days, and that many other animals had been killed.

"We all had to come. We couldn't leave you here alone at this difficult time. After all, the farm has been our home too," Alice said. "We don't know if we'll have another chance to say goodbye to Santa Virgínia and Lake Caracaranã. I imagine we won't run out of things to do in the next several days. The children are big now and can help."

No argument there—the children had indeed grown a lot. David had inherited my athletic build, and at nineteen, he was taller than me. He had his mother's delicate features and large, ever-smiling hazel eyes. Benjamin, who was almost three years younger, looked markedly different. He had straight black hair and dark skin and was a bit shorter and stocky. Everything about him evinced his indigenous heritage, except his eyes, which changed from light brown to greenish-gray depending on the light.

Antônio and Conceição's daughters had also changed radically. Taiana, who was just a few months younger than David, had blossomed beautifully and was now all woman. The mixture of Bulgarian and Wapishana ethnicities, combined with various other traits of undefined origin, had produced a distinct and lovely biotype: dishwater blond hair, green almond-shaped Oriental eyes that practically disappeared when she smiled, light skin tanned by constant exposure to the sun, shapely legs and a very feminine carriage, along with a somewhat athletic build earned from the years on the farm. All together, the result was a charming young woman of rare beauty.

"She's gorgeous!" As usual, Alice had guessed my thoughts. "Her sister Iara still has a bit of a baby face, but she also shows signs of turning into an exotic beauty. One thing is noticeable: they look lovely in casual clothes and sporty shoes, but I don't know if they'll look so good in heels. I don't think they were meant to be prima donnas."

Conceição was also gazing at the young people among us. She was bursting with pride. "Santa Virgínia can be proud. It helped raise these wonderful young people. We're so lucky!"

"They're what give me the strength to go on," Antônio said, in a weary voice. He was close to tears but quickly pulled himself together. "Friends, let's head to Caracaranã early tomorrow morning. We'll pick you up at your hotel at seven. I told the Correa de Melos we were going to visit their hotel. They said we can't stay there because the hotel is closed, so we'll sleep at Dona Benedita's. That's where we first met, eighteen years ago, remember? We'll leave Normandia the next day and head to Santa Virgínia. We'll stay there two nights. On our way back, we'll follow the trucks transporting the Nelore, horses, and dogs."

The young people kept the dinner table lively. It had been three years since they'd spent their vacation time together at the farm and many things had changed—starting with them. Taiana had begun college with a major in law, but after just one year she was so disillusioned with the field, especially after recent events, that she'd decided to switch.

David took a stab: "Veterinary medicine, right?"

"Precisely," Taiana replied. "What about you?"

"I'm a freshman at the university in Manaus. I'm majoring in business administration. But I'm thinking about something else too, maybe studying abroad. I'd like to go to the United States—that's become a tradition in the Hazan family."

"You'll need to speak fluent English," Taiana said.

"I'm already taking advanced classes at the Brazil-United States Cultural Institute, but I really need to make a lot more progress before I can pass the TOEFL," replied David, who obviously knew just where he was headed.

"I don't have any clue what I'll go into, but I'm working hard on my English too," Benjamin broke in. "My dad always says today's illiterate is someone who doesn't speak English and doesn't know his way around a computer."

"I've made up my mind. I'm going into medicine. But unlike my sister, who prefers animals, I'd rather deal with people," Iara teased.

The young people's talk was more interesting than ours and we paid more attention to it.

~~~~~~

Because there were so many Federal Police cars on highway BR-401, a certain nervousness hung in the air even before we entered the Raposa Serra do Sol reserve. Our convoy of three king-cabs was stopped for the first time shortly after we drove through the town of Bonfim. We were invited to step out and identify ourselves. Antônio explained that we were headed to Normandia and from there would go on to Santa Virgínia Fazenda to retrieve our belongings and collect the animals still on the farm. The deputy checked to see if we were armed, and then commented on the fact that we had women and young people with us. "It looks more like a picnic than an evacuation," he said with a smirk.

I was worried Antônio might talk back, so I spoke up before he could. I told the officer precisely where the farm was located and assured him, we'd be leaving in three days.

"After all, we have until April 30, right?" asked Taiana. The deputy sharply pointed out that non-Indians would not be allowed to enter the reserve without special permission much before that date. They'd also be restricted to federal and state highways and only allowed to travel on other roads with authorization. We couldn't complain about how the officers treated us. They were firm and strict but polite.

One of the federal agents recognized Roberto, who had been his professor at the Federal University of Roraima, and this helped things go smoother.

We were stopped a second time at the entrance to the reserve. The procedure was the same. It was obvious the officers had communicated with the first group via radio and were expecting our three-truck caravan. Once again, we were advised we couldn't carry any type of gun and should avoid contact with the Indians.

The rest of the trip was uneventful. There was hardly any traffic, so a little after noon, we pulled into the practically empty parking lot at Lake Caracaranã. We quickly noticed that all the doors to the chalets were wide open and there was no electricity. The beach was empty and, despite a nice wind, not a single colorful sail brightened the lake's green waters.

"Our best bet is to stay here tonight and enjoy the Cruviana once again," Antônio said, referring to the steady fresh breeze that provided respite from the heat, sometimes to the point of goose bumps.

"I'd rather leave," Conceição said unexpectedly. "It pains me deep in my heart. I've been coming here since I was little, and the place was always so full of life. I think I'll get sick if we stay here any longer."

We couldn't ignore her plea. We spent just a few minutes at the lake and then headed to Normandia. Though the city had doubled in size in recent years, it was still quite small. We had lunch at a cozy little diner and then took a hike into the Serra do Cruzeiro mountains since it was still early. We had a spectacular 360-degree view extending from the *lavrado* and Mount Roraima to the Maú River Valley.

By the time we reached the hotel in the late afternoon, we were worn out. Dona Benedita's home—where the Costa and Hazan families had met for the first time, eighteen years earlier—was now part of the inn owned by her neighbor, Dona Amélia. Dona Benedita, niece of the city's founder, had passed away some years earlier. Customer service at the small hotel was less personalized now but much more professional.

To everyone's surprise, the first person we saw, right at the front desk, was Joaquim Correa de Melo. He was nearly ninety but still had the same lively eyes. He was just a bit balder, but his eyebrows had turned completely white. When he saw Antônio, his eyes filled with tears. "My friend, my friend! My son told me you'd be coming today. Seeing you brings me a little joy in the saddest year of my life. Your father is so lucky he doesn't have to suffer this outrage." Joaquim wiped his tears and went on in a sad voice: "I was born on this land and always thought I'd be buried here, like my mother, Dona Cândida Menezes."

Joaquim was obviously shaken. He gave us a lengthy report of his sleepless nights obsessing over the loss of Fazenda Casa Branca, which included Lake Caracaranã and which, according to him, had been in his family since 1816.

"The only thing I've held onto from my beautiful land," he said, "are two bottles of lake water, six little bags of sand, and some leaves and branches from the cashew trees. I'm certain we could have come to an agreement with the Indians, but the government preferred to kick us off, and the courts obediently went along. To make it all seem legal, they offered us another piece of land, in exchange for Fazenda Caracaranã, but it's so remote you can't even get there. And the monetary compensation wouldn't cover the cost of re-settling. I once had as many as a hundred guests a day in the chalets at my inn, plus another two hundred at campground. My restaurant was packed on the weekends. None of that means anything to those people."

Joaquim wouldn't stop talking, but then his granddaughter walked in, obviously concerned when she saw his agitated state.

She deftly switched subjects and led him out of the hotel.

"They must be staying with relatives," Taiana said. "Their family is really important here in Normandia. His granddaughter goes to college with me. They're all real upset. Our law professor is always quoting Rui Barbosa: 'If justice is blind on one side, it isn't justice. It must see right and left equally.' This time, it only saw one side."

Joaquim's granddaughter came back in a little later. "My grandfather gets emotional when he talks about our lake," she said. "He's especially sensitive today because he's been remembering his friend, Mário Costa. He's been expecting you since yesterday, and he just hasn't stopped talking about the old days. Honestly, I don't think these emotions are good for him. He took a pill and now he should sleep through the night."

At daybreak, we climbed into our three pickups and took highway RR-319 out of Normandia toward Santa Virgínia. It had rained overnight, and the road wasn't maintained as well as it used to be, when the inn was open, and upkeep had been almost a daily routine. The muddy clay was dangerously slippery, and while this at least meant there wasn't any dust, we couldn't make good time. With the arrival of the rainy season, the *lavrado* had lost a bit of its usual predominantly yellow tone. It took us twice as long to get to Santa Virgínia. Two Federal Police cars were parked under some shady trees at the entrance. We recognized the same team of six who had stopped us the day before near the town of Bonfim. Even Roberto's student was there.

"We were expecting you," the deputy said. "We visited your land yesterday and got a nice welcome from your employees, Mr. Costa. That hasn't been the case on some of the other farms, where they wouldn't even let us in."

100

"My orders are that everyone should be made to feel welcome," Antônio said, "even the Indians. That's how it's been at Santa Virgínia Fazenda for the last seventy-six years."

"Are you armed?" the deputy asked, abruptly changing the subject.

"Officer, I answered that question yesterday," Antônio retorted. "We should be, but we're not, by force of the crazy rules of this game. In fact, yesterday you said it looked like we were going on a picnic, right? I'm here to pick up my forty head of cattle, my horses and dogs, and some personal belongings."

"We counted thirty head standing and five dead, as well as four horses and three German shepherds, one seriously injured," the deputy informed us.

"What did they die of? And the other five head? Did they evaporate into thin air? What's going on?" Antônio asked, incredulous.

Without answering his questions, the deputy went on: "We're here to protect you. We'll be close by throughout the two days you plan to be here. If necessary, we can talk by radio."

"You can come onto the premises. It'll be more comfortable for you," Antônio offered. I could tell he had calmed down a little.

"We'd better not," the deputy said. "We'll be close by and always have one ear on the radio. I recommend you all stay in a group and not leave the inn."

"I wanted to take a horse ride around the *lavrado*," said Taiana. She clearly didn't want to follow the deputy's orders. "It's the time of year when the wild horses show up."

"This is no time for outings, miss. We can't guarantee anyone's safety, especially on horseback and off the road. Don't complicate our lives while risking your own. Do your best to avoid contact with the Indians." The deputy sounded quite serious.

"At least we can go down to the beach and do some fishing tomorrow. The livestock trucks get here tomorrow afternoon. We'll head back to Boa Vista the day after tomorrow, bright and early, just after dawn. I've rented some space at a farm where we can keep the animals until we sell them," Antônio explained.

I asked what would become of the horses and dogs.

"I'm going to sell the Nelore, but I still don't know what I'm going to do with the horses. I've actually thought of setting them loose on the *lavrado*, but I don't think that's such a good idea, because they're crossbred, and I think it might interfere with the nature and blood of the *lavradeiros*. I have to figure something else out for them. I'll keep one dog—the next Sharo—at my home in Boa Vista. As to the other two, I haven't decided what I'm going to do," Antônio said.

Alice and I were tossing around the idea of taking the four horses and German shepherds to our cousins' farm in Maués, in the state of Amazonas, when Taiana arrived with the news that the injured dog had died.

The next day, we got busy preparing for the Costa family's definitive move. We gathered up all their records—including the famous book "The Jungle"—and a cardboard box stuffed with old photographs of Iolanda, the Wapishana, and of Mário Costa when he was young.

"They were so young and good-looking," Alice said. "Seeing these pictures, I can tell that Taiana and Iara look a lot like their grandma, although their complexions are lighter."

A larger cardboard box held a few pictures of Antônio when he was a child, almost always in the company of his father. There were also many newer photos of him with Conceição and the girls. At the bottom of the pile, we found a wooden box that had been carefully nailed shut.

"I haven't seen this in ages," Antônio said. "My father showed me this box before he died. He told me this would be our last reserve in hard times. He said he stored the first tiny diamond he'd ever found, in 1933, right in this box—for more than fifty years. But then he sold it because he needed money to travel to Rio de Janeiro and meet our Bulgarian friend, Ilia Deleff, the one who made a fortune selling giant crystals. When Ilia heard that my father had sold his valuable talisman, he insisted on replacing it. So he gave my father one of the diamonds he still had from his prospecting days. For the last twenty years, this little black box you see before you have lodged a new occupant, which, according to my father, is even more valuable than the first."

We were all eager to see the stone. After carefully pulling out the nails, Antônio delicately removed it from a small leather pouch. I could feel Alice holding her breath. To everyone's surprise, the diamond was very big indeed. Even to a non-expert's eyes, it was clearly a valuable stone.

Antônio was the most astonished of us all. He couldn't contain his excitement. "I thought it was just some ordinary old stone. But I remember this diamond. It's the biggest one we dug up, that first day we went prospecting along the lucky branch of the upper Tacutu River. I remember my father saying back then that the diamond was worth a fortune. I was eleven."

While Alice and I helped Antônio and Conceição, the young people romped around the beach that had been their playground when they were kids. In the late afternoon, repeating what we had done so many times over the years, back when the farm was our home, we met out on the tip of the stone to watch the sun go down. We were quiet as we bid a final farewell to our little paradise, trying to burn those last moments into our memories. Once again, we watched the familiar game of lights play out in that enchanted place. Right when the sun was about to plunge into the river's calm waters, an odd sound broke through the silence, bringing us back to reality: the transport trucks had arrived to pick up the animals.

Some of the old employees still lived on the farm, all from Genival's village. Although they would stay on after the Costa family left the reserve, they clearly weren't very happy—after all, they were losing their jobs. Things were bleak for them, partly because they'd always been harassed by the other Indians, who didn't approve of their working on the farm. Uncertainty loomed on their horizon nearly as much as on ours.

The next day, it took us several hours to load the animals. At the end, Antônio went to his parents' graves to say goodbye.

"I had the option of moving my parent's remains to Boa Vista, but I rejected the idea. This is where they belong; I'm sure they wouldn't want to leave. I hope they rest in peace. The Indians usually respect the dead." His eyes were brimming with tears.

It was close to noon when we said goodbye to the few employees who were left and would remain at the inn, and our convoy set off.

On our way out, we met up again with the Federal Police, who were discreetly parked there waiting for us. Antônio got out and handed the deputy the keys to the buildings. I watched him with a mix of admiration and pity. I knew what a difficult moment this was for my friend, who seemed to have shrunk in size and aged a dozen years in the past few days.

The road was in better shape because we hadn't had any more rain. Now the problem was the thick dust, which dramatically reduced a driver's visibility. A few miles along, not far from *tuxaua* Genival's village, we noticed a large group of Indians who were watching us pass by. We recognized some of the employees who had lived side by side with our families for years, so Antônio pulled over. We all got out. This final farewell hadn't been planned, but it was the most moving and spontaneous.

"I'd very much like to talk to *tuxaua* Gerônimo." Antônio surprised us all.

Someone went to get the *tuxaua*, but we waited so long that it became clear he wouldn't show. Fernando, my son Benjamin's brother, appeared instead. Once again, I took note of the striking resemblance between the twins, no longer boys but now young men. Their faces were almost identical, and they were nearly the same height, because Fernando had recently gone through a growth spurt. Were it not for their clothes, it would have been hard to tell them apart.

There wasn't time for anything else. Several squad cars pulled up and the deputy got out, gesturing nervously at Antônio and me. He called us over. "I thought you'd agreed to avoid contact with the Indians," he said gruffly. "That was our deal. Get out of here, now!"

It wouldn't do any good to explain we were saying goodbye to former employees, nor did we have time to tell them the complicated story of the twin brothers, Benjamin and Fernando. Given his order, we could do nothing but comply and leave.

So, without further farewells, our convoy of pickups, forced by the dust to keep a good distance apart, drove slowly back to the main road, followed by the two livestock trucks.

The last thing I saw in the rearview mirror was Fernando's face. It looked to me like he'd hoped to have one last word with his brother. I was driving and Benjamin was sitting behind me, so I couldn't look right at him. I fiddled with the rearview mirror until I could see the expression on his face. Like Fernando, he seemed bewildered and deeply disappointed.

〰〰〰〰〰〰〰〰〰〰〰〰

After this incident, we drove in silence for a long time, each of us lost in our own thoughts and memories.

"Antônio, do you really believe CONAB will be able to do the harvesting for you?" asked Roberto. The rice growers had signed an agreement according to which CONAB, the federal agricultural agency, would bring in their crops and then hand them over to the farmers, since everyone had been forced to abandon the reservation immediately, before harvest time.

"I don't know if this agreement will work in practice, but any little bit that can help compensate our losses will be most welcome. I'd rather get a fair value for my land, but that would be too much to ask," Antônio said in a discouraged voice.

We'd been making poor enough time with our five-vehicle convoy, but then the going got even slower as we joined a long line of vehicles moving off other farms. We were wrapped in a dust cloud that would have been much thicker had it not been for the steady wind that carried small particles of dirt off toward the mountains. A strong wind came along at one point and, as the air cleared a little, ahead of us we could see pickups, jeeps, harvesters, tractors, heavy irrigation equipment, trucks hauling cattle and other livestock, and even a few military vehicles.

The seemingly endless convoy crawled along the dirt road like a giant coffin. Progress was even slower when we crossed the rickety wooden bridges spanning the rivers and streams that cut through the plain. Much patience was needed. If we were lucky, we'd reach a paved road by early evening.

We returned to Manaus two days later. There was nothing else we could do for our friends. Some farmers held out for a few more days. Paulo César Quartiero refused to follow the verbal orders of the Federal Police agents who told him to leave and demanded to see a court order. It didn't do much good. The requested document was patiently handed over a few hours later. Not long after Quartiero left, Adolfo Esbell gave in as well—the last farmer to resist.

2015, six years later

Even though it's gotten easier to get from Manaus to Boa Vista by car in recent years, I haven't seen my friend Antônio much. He and Conceição drove to Manaus once, only to find themselves horrified by the big city traffic and swarms of people. The trip wasn't as pleasant as we would have liked, because it coincided with the unexpected death of the founder of our clan in the Amazon, Licco Hazan, my uncle. Antônio has a real aversion to long trips and I never managed to talk him and Conceição into traveling with us. I badly wanted to take them to Europe and maybe even Bulgaria, where we could look for his father's relatives and visit the museum that holds Ilia Deleff's huge crystals.

The Costa family still lives in the same house in Boa Vista, in the neighborhood of Paraviana, but they spend their weekdays at a new farm an hour and a half from the city, where they grow organic vegetables to sell in town. Antônio had finally returned to his father's original profession. It seems he's largely gotten over the trauma of losing Santa Virgínia. Although the new farm doesn't compare in size, much less in beauty, with Santa Virgínia, the family still maintains the rural lifestyle they all love. They have a few head of cattle and some horses and German shepherds. It's all vaguely reminiscent of the glorious days on the Surumu River.

When the Costas inaugurated their first vegetable greenhouse, Alice and I stayed there one weekend. Taiana went with us; she had just graduated from veterinary school. We rode about the countryside on horseback, like in the good old days.

We didn't come across a single *lavradeiro*, but Taiana said they still come around at a certain time of the year and it's easy to spot them. There has been growing interest in these horses, and Taiana has been thinking about taking groups of tourists out to watch them. Iara, who is more of a city-lover than her sister, is studying medicine in São Paulo. Whenever she comes back for a visit, she stops in Manaus and spends a few days with us. Our son, David, was awarded a scholarship and is realizing his dream of doing an MBA at Harvard.

Benjamin got his degree in engineering and now works with me. Of all of us, he's the one with closest ties to Roraima, and he visits Boa Vista quite often. Last year, he and Janaína, his birth mother, climbed Mount Roraima, something Alice and I would also like to do some day.

Our children still keep in close touch. This is easier now, thanks to modern means of communication, which are top quality and practically free, not like in the past.

Everyone in both families recently joined a text messaging group called Costa/Hazan Families, where we can exchange news whenever we want. I'd still rather talk by phone but I've got to admit that these new communications channels, where typing is more common than talking, are quite efficient.

One of the latest bits of news from the Costas is that Benjamin's twin brother, Fernando Macuxi, reached out to Antônio, because he wanted to meet up with his brother and get to know him better. I admit I asked myself if this was such a good idea. I can still remember the dejected looks on both the boys' faces when we said our hurried goodbyes at Santa Virgínia Fazenda, when the Federal Police pushed us to leave in a rush and the brothers didn't have time to exchange a single word. I shared my concern with Alice. Without a second's hesitation, she adamantly declared that we should encourage the blood brothers to have contact with each other. But it wouldn't be easy. Although Fernando was quite acculturated (he studied at the Federal University of Roraima), he had been raised in the small world of his tribe; his brother Benjamin, on the other hand, had enjoyed a cosmopolitan education in a globalized world. To add another layer of complication, one brother was a Catholic indigene and the other was Jewish.

Coincidentally or not, right when I was getting ready to talk things over with Benjamin, he told me he was planning another trip to Roraima. This time he intended to get to know his roots better and, at the very least, cross the Raposa Serra do Sol reserve on his way to Normandia, even if only via federal highways. He didn't say anything specific about looking up his brother Fernando or his birth mother, but I could tell it was part of his plans.

During our talk, I told him Fernando had recently contacted Antônio. The day after our conversation, Benjamin reached out to Antônio and was soon in touch with Fernando. Things moved surprisingly fast, and the Costa/Hazan group was soon talking about a possible trip to Raposa Serra do Sol, Lake Caracaranã, and the town of Normandia. It wasn't easy to coordinate all of our schedules with the rains that hit the *lavrado* between April and early October. The trip would no doubt be more enjoyable if we waited until the dry season, when life blossoms on the Brazilian savannah and the Indians are out hunting, fishing in the rivers, building and repairing their huts—which are made from clay, wood, and palm fronds—and visiting neighboring villages.

We knew we could make brief visits to Lake Caracaranã now, with the Indians' permission. Although the inn was closed, it would be nice to at least spend an afternoon there, because the place held so much meaning for us all. It would offer us a little solace, since we had no hopes of being able to leave the main highway and visit Santa Virgínia without a special permit from FUNAI, and that was unlikely, especially for former owners.

And so, after many long conversations, on Monday, October 26, 2015, Benjamin, Alice, and I left Manaus early in the morning in our double-cab four-wheel drive pickup, hardy enough for the slippery roads of Raposa Serra do Sol. We reached Boa Vista seven hours later. Despite our best efforts in planning the trip, not everybody who wanted to was able to join us. We knew David and Iara wouldn't be able to come, because he couldn't afford to miss school and she was doing an important fellowship at a hospital in São Paulo. Alice missed the excursion too, as Conceição wasn't in good health, and my wife decided to stay behind with her good friend at the Costa home in Boa Vista. With this additional absence, our group was small: Benjamin, Taiana, Antônio, and me. We decided we could all fit in my truck.

It took us only three hours to get to Caracaranã, since the longest stretch of the road (about 60 miles) had been paved. As planned, we got there around noon and met Fernando Macuxi at the entrance to the former inn.

The first moments were a bit awkward, but Fernando soon had the conversation flowing, and the atmosphere relaxed. It was hard to believe the twins were finally together, really talking for the first time ever. In fact, it seemed like they'd never been separated in their twenty-three years of life. Fernando told us how some things had improved for the Indians after the rice growers and farmers left the reserve, but other things had gotten much worse, despite federal government promises.

"We don't have any assistance. We aren't familiar with the rice growers' advanced agricultural technology. We need technical assistance to improve and boost our production, which currently comes from small fields. There simply aren't any green fields of irrigated rice anymore. Everything has dried up and isn't producing," Fernando admitted. "A lot of people left the reserve and now live on the periphery of Boa Vista in poor conditions. Regrettably, some have found only sub-standard jobs at landfills, and some girls have turned to prostitution to survive."

"We've got a few former employees from Santa Virgínia working on our new farm," Antônio said.

"My mother, Janaína, still lives here on the reserve, but Gerônimo, my stepdad, spends most of his time in Boa Vista. He's old and worn out. Back then, he promised everyone the world, and he also got a lot of folks against him. Now they want him to make good on his promises."

We were familiar with all this. After the rice producers and other farmers had left Raposa Serra do Sol, Gerônimo had become the leading representative of the Indigenous Council of Roraima in the village. Because promises went unfulfilled, and the state government also wasn't investing in health, education, and infrastructure, he had never been able to cement his leadership and had soon lost his reputation in the small village. I imagined this would open the way for young Fernando.

"I took my grandfather Genival's advice and studied hard. This year I'll get my degree in business administration from the Federal University of Roraima, and then I'll come back home," he said. "I want to help my people improve their lives. It's no use owning land if you can't feed your children. Despite what the rest of the world thinks, we Indians aren't going back to living off game, wearing spathes from a buriti palm tree on our feet, and going around with bare behinds. Grandpa Genival understood this much better than FUNAI. He always said our world changes with yours, and that integration is more productive than separation," Fernando said, venting his frustrations.

Benjamin agreed with him. "That's not what happens here, or what Brazilian public policy preaches. The idea that holds sway in Brazil right now is a romantic vision that ignores the fact that in order to enjoy health, education, entertainment, food, television, electricity, roads, bridges, and the internet—and still preserve their culture—Indians need to work and produce wealth like other Brazilians."

Indeed. You just had to look around you. Little remained of Joaquim's chalets or the packed restaurant of yesteryear. We were the only visitors. Only one other car, carrying two passengers, came through that day. They paid the cheap entrance fee, stayed less than an hour, and went on their way. Caracaranã was in a sorry state and offered absolutely no amenities. The only thing you could do there was take a quick dip in the crystal-clear water or snap a pretty picture.

The day rushed by. We watched the sunset once again. Indifferent to the other changes around there, the sky was as spectacular as ever. There was no moon, and just before full darkness set in, I suggested we head to Normandia, where we could spend the night at Dona Amélia's inn. But Fernando insisted on staying, and Benjamin and Taiana decided to stay too. We had brought hammocks along, so we all could have stayed, but Antônio discretely signaled to me that he'd rather leave the young people alone. We left them some sandwiches and water and hit the road.

Back in the car, Antônio explained: "Oleg, these three young people can make a big difference to the future of Raposa Serra do Sol. Benjamin and Taiana have really hit it off with Fernando, and I'm almost certain they'll want to help him with what the future may bring. They'll be more comfortable without us around. After all, like me, they're mixed ethnicity, born and raised here. Who knows, maybe this whole story will have a happier ending someday."

"It's too early to reach any conclusions, but one thing did call my attention: I felt a little spark between Taiana and Fernando." As soon as the words were out of my mouth, I regretted it.

Antônio laughed and added: "Fernando confided in me that his grandfather, Genival, was always secretly in love with my mother. Two generations later, maybe this passion has been re-ignited between the grandchildren of Iolanda, a Wapishana, and Genival, a Macuxi. Who knows, it might work out this time around."

The lights of Normandia were twinkling ahead of us.

~~~~~~~~~~~~~~~~~~~~~~~~~

I was driving through heavy traffic in downtown Manaus, my head in the clouds, so I didn't pay much attention when my phone notified me of a new WhatsApp message. Another notification soon followed, and then my phone started dinging away. I realized something must be up on one of the three groups my children had convinced me to join (somewhat against my will). I wasn't a very active participant in the groups I belonged to: Hazan Cousins, Costa/Hazan Family, and Manaus Tennis Community. Then the phone actually rang, and from the corner of my eye I saw that David was trying to get through. I'd just turned onto Eduardo Ribeiro Avenue, where traffic was especially heavy, so it was hard to pull over and answer. The phone stopped ringing. I wasn't far from my office by then, so I just kept going. One message after another was coming through, and for the first time that day, a bit of worry crept in. I'd just gotten out of the car when the phone rang again. It was Alice this time, and I managed to pick up.

"You never answer your phone! Everyone wants to talk to you. Even Antônio has called from Boa Vista, and David from the United States, and you don't answer. Didn't you see the flood of messages on WhatsApp? Look at your phone!" She quit scolding me and hung up. Since Alice didn't sound worried or nervous, I figured there was no reason for alarm. As I stepped into my office, I opened the app and saw there were thirty-seven new messages on the Costa/Hazan Family group, and more were pouring in. I began reading:

Taiana: Fernando and I want to let you all know we're engaged.

Iara: OMG! Congratulations, sis and Fernando. When's the wedding?

Benjamin: Congrats! What took u so long?

Taiana: We haven't set the date, but it'll be in 2016.

Alice: We're so happy for you!

David: Fernando, promise you'll take good care of my sister!

Conceição: Congratulations! But you could have given us a little hint…

Antônio: This is the best news we've had in a long time. We want grandkids!

Taiana: Don't worry, dad, the first one's already on the way.

I felt tears come to my eyes, like the day at Domodedovo when I met my mother again after so many years. I found a chair, sat down, and typed:

Oleg: Congratulations! Mazel Tov! That night at Lake Ca-
          racaranã, Antônio and I could tell Benjamin was go-
          ing to be a third wheel. We're all very happy for you!

In a little while, a message came in from Antônio:

Antônio: Oleg, my brother, before my first grandchild is born,
          it's time for us to make that trip to
          Bulgaria, the one we've been talking about for years.
          We'll meet up with your mother. I want to visit Bul-
          garia and spend some days in Moscow.

Glossary

balata
A kind of rubber produced by trees of the *Sapotaceae* species. Used to make funeral urns and adornments.

Canaimé
An evil spirit.

capitão de aldeia
Individual assigned to an indigenous village to represent the Portuguese Crown and enforce its interests. His duties included overseeing the exploitation of indigenous peoples as slaves.

Cruviana
The goddess of the wind among some Indian tribes. During the night, she transforms herself into a breeze and seduces men who are passing through.

curumim
Young boy; male baby.

FUNAI
National Indian Foundation. The Brazilian government agency in charge of indigenous affairs.

INCRA
National Institute for Colonization and Agrarian Reform, a federal agency charged with implementing land reform and managing public lands.

lavrado
A savannah-like region in the State of Roraima with a unique ecosystem.

tuxaua
Indigenous chief

About the Author

Ilko Minev was born in 1946 in the comunist Bulgaria, but after living in Brazil for more than forty years, he feels like a native Brazilian.

Because of his contributions to the society where he lives in the Amazon, he was named an Honorary Citizen of Manaus. He fled Bulgaria as a political dissident and received asylum in Belgium, where he studied economics before moving to Brazil. He began writing at the age of 66, after retiring from his career as a business executive. His books offer portraits of notable events in history and his own life, transcending nationality while embracing the influence of his Jewish-Bulgarian roots and his love for Brazil.

www.ingramcontent.com/pod-product-compliance
Lightning Source LLC
Chambersburg PA
CBHW021928170626
46807CB00007B/3023